Father, Ford, $5 a Day

The Mullers from Missouri

Sherry A. Wells, author

Randy Bulla, illustrator

Lawells Publishing
Ferndale, Michigan
© 2003

Books by Sherry A. Wells
Michigan Law for Everyone, 5 editions through 2002
Warm and Wonderful, Stepmothers of Famous People

Published by
   Lawells Publishing, *www.lawells.net*
   PO Box 1338, Royal Oak MI 48068
Educators and librarians, contact us for teaching tools

Publishers Cataloging-in-Publication

Wells, Sherry A.
The Mullers from Missouri; Father, Ford, $5 a Day *series.*

Families came from all over the country and the world
to Detroit in the 1910s and 1920s to build cars and
built a diverse city. Twelve-year old Herb learns that
the railroad cut Dad's job and that means leaving
Missouri to move to Detroit where his uncle works for
Ford Motor Company. Herb will lose his newspaper
route. Will he get another job in Michigan? Will they
be as free to explore and play? Will the family finally
get their own car?

[1. Family life—Michigan—Fiction. 2. Family life—
Missouri—Fiction. 3. Detroit (Michigan)— Fiction.
 4. Depressions—1929 —Fiction 5. Automobiles—
Fiction. 6. Humorous stories—Fiction.]   I. Title.

L.C. No. 2003093642
[Fic]
ISBN 0-934981-11-6 (lib.bdg.)

Printed by Thomson-Shore, Inc., Dexter, Michigan
On recycled paper

Dedication

To Herb, his sister, Juanita, and brother, Richard—
"the kids across the street," and to Amanda, my kid.

Personal Acknowledgments

I just finished reading the Little House books to my
daughter when our neighbor, Herb Muller, gave me a
copy of his submission to Old Timers tell it like it was,
the book of anecdotes published by the Ferndale
Historical Society. My mind saw chapters in those five
pages.

I met several times with all three of them, "So they
don't tell lies about me," said Dick, to hear about what
children did back then. I also called Walt, in Florida
now, to give him a chance to defend himself.

Don Daly, Georgette Yezbick Daly, and June Waugh
Kotlarek, whose stories were in the Old Timers book,
gave me details and drawings for a fuller picture.

I owe a great deal to friends: Clint Williams, a "Ford
Man" and very much his own man, and a benefactor;
Sylvan Zaft, PhD. and *amiko,* who edited and encouraged;
Meg Coughlin, another personal aider and abettor, once
employed by Ford as a lawyer and who still drives Fords;
the SCBWI—the Society of Children's Book Writers and
Illustrators, and the members who taught, critiqued,
praised and encouraged.

To Amanda, my assistant editor, and Mrs. Stafford's
4th graders at John F. Kennedy School, Ferndale School
District, who helped polish the book as I read it aloud.

And, *in memoriam,* to Laura Ingalls Wilder, whose
enjoyable way of learning the "real people" history of
our country through her books inspired me to write and
to enlist others to write in this series about another
frontier—just as new to the children of its age. This book,
like those of hers, creates an accurate, and only
somewhat fictionalized, representation of the people,
places and times.

Research Acknowledgements

Benson Ford Research Center, Dearborn, Michigan,
    and especially the Reminiscences of William Klann.
Detroit Public Library and its Burton Historical
Collection and National Automotive History Collection.
Ferndale Historical Society and its museum
The Internet: Harvey Houses

Bibliography

The Detroit Almanac, edited by Peter Gavrilovich and
    Bill McGraw, Detroit Free Press, 2001.
Ferndale 1918-1943, A Century of Progress in 25
    Years, Harvey S. Jacobs, Publisher, 1943.
Ferndale of Yesteryear, by Maurice F. Cole, Emefcee
    Publications, 1971.
The First Fifty Years, an informal history of the Detroit
    Zoological Park, 1974, The Detroit Zoological
    Society. Loaned me by my cousin Frank Loftus,
    City of Detroit Historiographer, from his personal
    collection.
Old Timers tell it like it was, Ferndale Historical
    Society, 1987.
Pronouncing Gazeteer of the World, 1905.

All three books about the Ford Motor Company by
    Allan Nevins and Frank Ernest Hill:
    Ford: The Times, The Man, The Company 1863-1915
    Ford: Expansion and Challenge 1915-1933
    Ford: Decline and Rebirth 1933-1962

Table of Contents

Juanita
Herbert, Richard and Walter 1921

Photo and labeling courtesy of Herbert Muller

1. Leave Missouri?!

Herb came in the back door. Dad and Mom sat at the kitchen table talking in low voices. They didn't hear him come in.

"It's certain, Clara," Dad said. "They'll be closing the Oronogo station, too. Otto says there are no jobs with the railroad that he knows about." Uncle Otto Mueller had an important position for the St. Louis-San Francisco Railway. That's how Dad came to be the stationmaster. They'd moved here in 1915 when Herb was five.

Mom twisted her apron in her lap. "In Tom's last letter, he said there were still more jobs at the Ford factory. Perhaps..."

Herb held his breath. Move away from Oronogo? But this was home for as long as he could remember. He knew he'd been born in St. Louis. And then Walt was born in Florida. But Dick was just a baby when they came to this town and that was seven years ago. More than half of Herb's life and nearly all of what he

1

could remember was spent in Oronogo. All of his friends were here.

And what about his job delivering the *Kansas City Star*? He'd have to give up that, too.

Mom always read Uncle Tom's letters out loud. Herb groaned inside as he remembered that in his last letter Uncle Tom again suggested Dad get a job where he worked. "Herman could earn even more than the $5 a day that I got when I started there in 1914."

"Would you be willing to leave Missouri?" Dad asked.

Leave Missouri? But that meant leaving Grandma and aunts and uncles and cousins, and the big family Christmas dinners and summer picnics in St. James and St. Louis.

"I believe a city could offer our children more opportunities," Mom answered. "And you know how close I feel to Tom. He was almost like a father to me. Our children have cousins there, too."

Only two. One boy a year older than he was and a girl almost as young as Juanita.

"Well, then," Dad said, "write to Tom and tell him I'm ready to take him up on his offer. You and the children can join me after school is out."

Dad leaned back and saw Herb standing just inside the back door. Herb let out his breath and tried to say, "Hi, Dad," but words wouldn't come out.

"I guess you heard what we were talking about," Dad said. "Well, you're the oldest, so I'm counting on you to help take care of things after I leave for Detroit."

"I'll take care of the family, Dad," Herb said. "I promise I'll take very good care of them."

The whole family went to the Oronogo station to see Dad get onto the train. Although Dad had boarded up the station himself, the railroad men knew when he was leaving and stopped in Oronogo for him.

2

"Well, I guess I get to be the last passenger picked up at this station," Dad said. He managed about half a grin. Herb tried to grin back at least a three-quarters grin but he barely matched Dad's attempt.

"Remember that I've put Herb in charge of helping your mother with all of you," Dad said, as he set Juanita down next to Herb.

Walt and Dick looked more stunned now than when they first heard the news. This time they didn't grumble when Dad said he'd put Herb in charge. I guess it's starting to sink in for all of us.

They all watched as Dad's train moved away. Dad stood at the back of the caboose and kept waving even as the train went around a bend.

For the next few months, Herb stored memories while he helped Mom fill boxes. As he delivered the *Star*, he looked at the town as he had never looked at it before. In his heart, he was saying goodbye to it all.

Oronogo was a mining town, named for "ore or no go," Dad said. They lived almost on top of the mines. Dick and his friends used tailings–the small pieces of lead left over after mining operations, as ammunition for their slingshots. Most of the time they shot at tin cans, birds and rabbits.

Herb had shot one bird. As he held its lifeless yet still warm body in his hand, he realized it would never warble a pretty song again or stretch its colored feathers and fly. He vowed to never shoot at another living thing.

Where there weren't mines, there were farms. They had all they wanted to eat of sweet potatoes, which were Herb's favorite, and corn, bought from the farmers down the road. Despite their small lot, they had their own chickens, which meant fresh eggs every day.

The farms were well-stocked with cats, too. Juanita knew that if she walked down the road in the morning,

"Uncle Jimmy" would give her a soft kitten or two to take home. She brought out her little iron doll bed for them to sleep on. She dressed them up and sat them down for tea with her dolls.

Usually Mom yelled at whichever of her sons was closest to "Take every one of them back. Four children are quite enough to feed and care for." This spring, Herb made sure that Juanita's picks of this season's litter were back to Uncle Jimmy's well before supper each evening.

Also in time for supper, Herb knew where to look for Walt and Dick. The boys and their friends had a clubhouse in the hayloft of the barn behind the grocery store. They had dug a hollow in the loose hay in a corner to hold their secret meetings—away from little sisters and other girls.

If they weren't up there plotting mischief, he knew to look along the banks of the creek. They'd be catching crawdads for the fun of waving them at those same girls.

One afternoon, Herb took Dad's Brownie camera with them when he took Juanita out for a walk across one of the many hilly fields. He saw a stile straddling the fence between it and the field next to it and lifted her onto the top.

"Smile for Daddy."

Although it was barely higher than his waist, Juanita began to whimper.

"I'm scared."

Herb snapped the photograph, and then helped her down.

Would they have as much room and freedom to explore in a big city like Detroit? Would he be able to get another job? Or would those jobs all be taken by other boys already there? He still had nearly all the money he'd earned — there wasn't much to spend it on in Oronogo.

Mom rented a truck to take their belongings to the train station at Webb City. Herb neatly wrote what was in each box on the top and one of the sides. Their neighbor, Mr. Farrier, and Herb stacked the big boxes and furniture onto the front porch to be loaded into the truck. Herb instructed Walt and Dick to carry out the smaller boxes.

To Herb's surprise, Walt and Dick didn't object much to his orders. During the past months, he'd overheard them imagining what life would be like living in a city as big as St. Louis. They bragged about it to their friends, but Herb was sure he heard some sadness in their voices as they said their good-byes. Their minds, too, were on all the changes the move would bring.

Everyone they knew in the town stopped by to see Mom. Some of them handed her envelopes. They asked her to be sure to give her husband their thanks for all his help.

"And we thank you for yours, too, Clara. You're going to have some mighty thankful neighbors up there." All of them said things like that.

2. Riding the Rails

"All a-*board*," the conductor called.

Mom led five-year old Juanita to their seats. Herb shepherded his brothers to the section across the aisle.

After they settled into their seats, Mom said, "This will probably be our last train trip for a long time. Now that your Dad doesn't work for the railroad, we can't get free passes."

"But we'll have our own car instead," Herb said. That was a sure thing with Dad now working for the Ford Motor Company. Uncle Tom wrote that his Model T was manufactured at the plant where he worked. Still, Herb would miss the train rides.

"Dickie, remember our trip to California?" Herb asked.

"I do!" Walt answered instead. "I remember the Petrified Forest. And the Grand Canyon. And the Indians dancing. And the things they made to sell to travelers."

The trip to visit Mom's family took four days.

"I remember how the Indian families moved everything they had on a travois," Herb said. "They didn't have a freight car like we do. Just those two poles they strapped to their horse with the ends dragging on the ground."

They traveled in a Pullman car that time. At night, the porters made up the beds. They pulled the upper berth down from the ceiling and turned the seats so that they made the lower berth. They spread out sheets and blankets and neatly tucked them in.

"Mom, are we going to eat at Harvey Houses on this trip?" Herb asked.

There had been Harvey Houses at every big station. Each had a newsstand and a big glass display case full of boxes of cigars. There was a high counter with chairs that swiveled so the customer could climb up, turn to face the counter and, when he was done eating, swivel halfway around and get off.

It was Herb's job to run ahead and stretch out over five seats to save them for his family.

"No. There are no Harvey Houses east of Kansas," Mom said, as the train's whistle began to blow.

The engine strained to pull the train cars out of the station. Puffs of dark gray coal smoke raced from the top of the engine towards the caboose. The train settled into a steady rhythm.

"I am going to miss Miss Blanche very much," Juanita said.

"I will miss her, too," Mom sighed. "She's been a life saver."

Miss Blanche was Mr. Farrier's grown daughter and she still lived at home. She treated Juanita as if she were her own daughter, sewing clothes for her and having her over for little tea parties.

"With three boys, goodness knows I don't have time for tea parties," Mom complained to Dad. More than once she said, "Troublemakers all of them."

"What I'm going to miss most about Oronogo is..." began Walt.

"Tornadoes." Dick finished the sentence.

They fled to the neighbor's cyclone cellar twice when the gigantic black funnel clouds were sighted.

"No. Not tornados," Juanita objected. "May Day baskets. Mom, will they have May Day in Detroit?"

"There's a first day of May everywhere, Silly..." Dick said.

"Stop calling me Silly," Juanita pouted.

Dick grinned, "...just as there's a Fourth of July everywhere." Dad caught them on that joke only once.

Filling baskets with flowers to hang on people's doors, knock and run away had to be something everybody would do on May Day, whether in Missouri or in Michigan. It was better than harmless fun. It was helpful fun.

He knew that when the older boys took apart a wagon and put it back together on top of the livery stable on Halloween, it wasn't helpful, but it was funny.

Another Halloween, the bigger boys shoved and dragged a cow up the stairs to the second floor of the two-room school.

Because tipping over outhouses was another favorite prank, Dad used two strong boards to brace theirs so those same boys wouldn't tip it over.

"I hope they have shivarees, too," Walt grinned. "Remember when the Williams boy got married? That was lots of fun. We sure made an awful ruckus."

Between them, they remembered three weddings. After each one, all the children pounded on pans and pails outside the house of the newlywed couple. Each groom stashed a bag of candy by his door and flung it out by the handfuls. The children gleefully grabbed it up and scampered off.

"Yeah, but Juanita got too scared for *her* wedding!" Dick teased.

Their church had planned a Tom Thumb wedding and Juanita was to be the "bride."

"I was afraid there were going to put me *in* the barrel," she pouted.

"No, they were just going to stand you on it so everyone could see you and Johnny," Mom said, sending "that look" to Dick.

"Mom, can I go hunting in Michigan? I wonder if they have bigger game than Missouri has." Every time he collected some money, Walt sent away for hunting stuff from the catalogs. He sighed. "But I don't guess there'd be any hunting in a big city."

Their train rushed past the next station, barely slowing to toss out the mailbag. Dad often took his children to the station with him, to give Mom some peace and quiet. Many times they watched him hang a big mailbag on the hook for the oncoming train. The postal clerk on the train threw the bag of mail for Oronogo onto the ground. Dad picked it up and tossed it into a cart. Sometimes he let one of them ride in the cart with the mailbag.

"What's in there, J. H.? Mail?" one passerby asked.

"Female," Dad grinned. Juanita was in the cart that time.

Every time the phone rang with one long ring and two short rings, Juanita chimed back, "I want to talk to Daddy!" If there was just one ring, the operator was signaling for all those on the party line to pick up their phones. Any other set of rings meant the call was for someone else in the neighborhood and they weren't supposed to pick it up and listen.

In one letter from Uncle Tom, he told about having his own telephone line plus running water, indoor plumbing and electricity. The Mullers had running water, too, though it was only one faucet on a pipe coming out of the ground outside. Mom had a water pump in the kitchen. Instead of an indoor toilet, they had the outhouse. On extremely cold days, you did what you had to do very quickly.

Their house was lit by gaslights, which meant the tank at the base of each light needed to be kept filled and the specially treated mantle cloth adjusted just right. Mom still managed to read to them every night around the table.

The train rocked in time with the clicks of its wheels on the rails.

3. From Grandmother's House We Go

"St. James," the conductor called.

In merely two hours, they arrived to visit Grandmother once more before going on to Detroit. Dad once showed them where St. James was on a railway map — a little more than halfway between Oronogo and St. Louis.

Grandfather and Grandmother Muller came from the same town in Germany when they were young. They married in America, and then came to St. James where they established a furniture business. Herb barely remembered Grandfather, who died when Herb was five.

Herb knew that their grandparents had been well known and well liked in St. James from the way people spoke to Grandmother at church and as they walked with her during visits.

As they went through the gate, they could see that Grandmother was under the pine tree in her black rocking chair waiting for them. They lined up.

"Herbert, you have grown so much since Christmas. You are as tall as a man. Your father said he left you in charge of helping your mother with the man's work around the house. And did you do so?

"Valter, have you been staying out of trouble?" Grandmother always pronounced *w* like a *v*.

"That is how we said his name in the old country," Grandmother once told them. "It is hard to learn a new language when you are already 21."

She'd also explained how differently the last name was pronounced and spelled in Germany. It sounded more like mule-er. With a strange sound to the *u*.

Grandmother showed Herbert how she still signed her name Müller, with the two dots above the *u*. Uncle Otto spelled it Mueller to help people pronounce it closer to the original way. Dad was used to hearing "Mull-er" but he said it didn't bother him.

Dick's turn was next.

"Richard, have you been letting your brothers and sister eat, too? My, I do not understand where all the food goes. You should be as fat as a pig at the fair."

"And little Nita. You have grown so big now. I hope you will find friends in Detroit for your tea parties."

Grandmother smiled a big smile at them all and they were free to go.

Herb hoped there were cookies waiting for them. Aunt Clara, who had the same first name as Mom, baked the most delicious anise cookies. They smelled like licorice candy but tasted even better. Sometimes she put just an inch of Grandmother's dandelion wine in their glasses for them to have with their cookies.

"Herbert," Aunt Clara called out. "Here are some cookies to take with you to Uncle Albert's. I want *you* to carry them so your cousins get some, too," she twinkled at Dick.

The three boys scampered through the backyard and across the alley to play with their cousin Albert.

As soon as their girl cousins saw the boys, they went to Grandmother's to entertain Juanita.

All too soon, Grace and Agnes came back.

"Grandmother says it is time for dinner," Grace announced.

As they passed Grandmother's parlor, Herb saw Grandfather's blue Civil War uniform hanging as if it were in a museum, with his saber on the wall behind it. The smell of polish was strong and the dark wood furniture shone warmly.

Grandmother's piano was nearby. Whenever Aunt Clara sat down at the piano, Herbert asked for The Star Spangled Banner. She played the song with strong fingers and everyone sang loudly and joyfully.

"I will always feel that I have lived in the Age of Invention," Grandmother said over dinner. "The telegraphy was considered wonderful but when the telephone was put to use, that was marvelous. The wireless messages have always been a mystery to me.

"Then came the phonograph. How well I remember when Albert was in his early twenties. What a surprise he gave the family when he brought in his phonograph and the wax cylinder records. We could hear Lincoln's speech at Gettysburg as if we were there. And Deutschland Über Alles. Although that has not been popular since the Great War."

"Don't gulp down that food!" Mom looked at Dick. "We have two hours before we have to be back on the train for Saint Louis."

"Wonders never cease." Grandmother looked around at them all. "And now you are going to Detroit where your father is helping to make the automobile. I remember the first horseless carriage which I saw. With a splutter and spitting, it came rushing down the streets, causing much amusement. And now we rush through the world in everything imaginable on wheels from a Tin Lizzie to a magnificent limousine."

After dinner, they were allowed to play only in Grandmother's yard.

"And stay clean!" Mother emphasized with her pointer finger.

All too soon, Herb heard Mom say, "And now, Mother, we have to hurry." Mom looked at each of her children like a mother duck counting beaks.

Grandmother hugged each of them longer than usual. Aunt Clara handed them a package of her cookies, "to eat on the train *tomorrow*."

Uncle Otto met them at the station in Saint Louis.

"Clara, I am so sorry there were no railroad jobs for Herman. You know I did what I could. But I have heard very good things about Detroit. I'm sure you have, too, from your brother." He looked at his nephews. "Robert will miss you boys. But I still work for the railroad. We can come to visit you in Detroit."

"I wish we had time to visit Shaw's Garden once more," Mom said. "Those orchids are incredibly beautiful." Mom's favorite color was the delicate faint purple of an orchid. She had a shirtwaist of that color and it looked beautiful on her.

On visits to St. Louis, they went to Forest Park for picnics. Once, hot air balloons meandered halfway up the sky while they ate their picnic lunch. They could easily get Mom to tell them again about the St. Louis Exposition that had been built on the same vast grounds that enclosed both Forest Park and the zoo.

The St. Louis Exposition had been a grand event. Mom was a young woman then but hadn't met Dad yet. Some boys held the fence up so she could crawl under it and get in without paying. She still had a small bottle of perfume she bought there. She told them about how the newspapers boasted that the Exposition had the first ice cream cone, and the first hot dogs, and the first iced tea.

The proud St. Louis Art Museum, guarded by the statue of St. Louis the Crusader, had also been built for the Exposition. Would Detroit have a zoo and a museum and beautiful park?

The family ate supper at Uncle Otto's. The boys shared Robert's room and Mom and Juanita shared the guest room. The sun woke Herb just before Mom knocked at the bedroom door. He was reaching for his clothes, which he had folded and placed at the foot of the bed the night before.

"Herb, get your brothers up. Don't let them dawdle," she called.

The train whistled as it came to the bridge that spanned the wide Mississippi River. They were leaving St. Louis and all of Missouri behind.

4. The Big City by Night

From St. Louis it was mostly fields through Illinois and Indiana. By the time they reached Ohio, it was getting dark. They had eaten Aunt Clara's cookies hours earlier.

Throughout most of the trip, Mom talked with Ida Myers. Mrs. Myers was also leaving Oronogo to go to Michigan. Her grown sons had gone ahead. Carl was working for Ford, too.

Years before, Mrs. Myers' husband ran off and left her in Oronogo with three children to raise by herself. She did it by taking in washings. Somehow, every time she returned from buying food for her own household she always managed to have a banana or other piece of fruit to give to Dick.

"It's my turn for the pillow." Dick grinned and grabbed it from Juanita.

"We're not taking turns," Juanita whined. "Grandma Myers said I could nap on it. Give it back to me."

Mom glared at Dick as she reached into the large cloth bag she brought. Dick pressed himself back into his seat.

Mom lifted out the Edgar Rice Burroughs book from his Men from Mars series, which she was reading to them in the evenings. They liked those better than the Tarzan book he wrote.

"Whew." Dick breathed again as Mom started to read aloud.

When Mom read to them, it not only calmed them down but she seemed to relax as well.

It was very late that night when the train slowed for their station in Detroit. Mom asked Herb to wake up his brothers. She gently nudged Juanita, who was still clutching the pillow.

Dick was sleeping with his face towards the window. An instant after he opened his eyes, he yelled.

"It's snowing!" He jumped up and headed toward the door, just ahead of Mom's attempt to restrain him. "Hey Walt! Herb! Look at that!"

"In May? Did we get on a train to Alaska by mistake?" Walt pressed his nose to the window. "I don't see any polar bears or igloos."

"Maybe they haven't let out school yet here." Herb suggested with a sly smile. "Can't plant crops in the frost, so I'll bet that we'll be back in school until spring gets up here."

Dick turned around. His eyebrows met at the bridge of his nose to confer about that dreadful possibility.

"Where's Daddy?" Juanita tried to see out the window.

"I see him over here, Nita." Mrs. Myers lifted Juanita onto her lap so she could peer out.

"There's Uncle Tom with him." Mom smiled, as she wrapped a shawl around Juanita.

Herb handed Walt two suitcases and took the larger two himself.

Dad was right by the door to help Mom down the last step. He squeezed her with one arm around her waist and leaned down to pick up Juanita with the other arm. Then he took Mom's bag.

Mom and Uncle Tom gave each other a quick hug but looked into each other's eyes for several seconds afterwards. She let out a long contented sigh.

As she walked between Dad and her brother, she stepped lightly and with more energy than Herb ever recalled seeing.

Herb waited at the top of the steps until Mrs. Myers let herself down them. He saw Dick trying to catch a snowflake on his tongue.

Carl Myers approached his mother as Herb stepped down.

"We'll see you soon, Ida," Mom said.

"I'll get my pillow from you then, Juanita, dear," Mrs. Myers said.

"My Tin Lizzie is over here." Uncle Tom led the way to the parking area.

The snow stayed a bit longer on the top of Model T and contrasted with the blackness of the automobile's roof.

Walt and Dick climbed into the back seat. Dad lifted up Juanita until her feet touched the floor and Dick pulled her in. As Herb started to climb in, Dad put a hand on his shoulder.

"In her letters to me, your mother wrote often about how you helped her organize what needed to be brought and what needed to be given away. And," he grinned, "the many times you took those three out for walks. I'm proud of you. You made it less hard on me to be so far away."

Herb stood a bit straighter and smiled. Then he climbed in and took the luggage from Dad, sliding one piece at a time on the floor between their feet and the back of the front seat.

Uncle Tom gave the car just one crank and it started right up. He climbed in. "Didn't get too cold yet. It's good that the train was right on time."

"I'm sorry you won't be able to see much of the city on account of the dark," Uncle Tom said as he drove away from the station. "We're planning to go to Belle Isle for a picnic on Sunday and I'll give you a special tour down Woodward then."

They drove in almost complete darkness for a few minutes until Uncle Tom turned onto a wide street.

"This is Woodward," Uncle Tom said. "The Main Street of Detroit."

They looked out the windows at the silent structures lined up on either side of them.

"Now here's something you can see. It's where your Dad and I work — the Ford Motor Company." Uncle Tom pointed out acres and acres of buildings with hundreds of lighted windows and tall smokestacks exhaling gray smoke. "Since we're working three shifts, it's always busy."

"Yes," Dad agreed. "It feels as though we're always busy, too. Most of us alternate two weeks on each of the three shifts. Few men wanted to give up their families entirely, which is what working only afternoons or midnights felt like. Actually," he chuckled and looked at Mom, "it was the wives who complained."

Uncle Tom resumed, "When the Highland Park plant was built ten years ago, the main part of it was the largest structure under one roof in the entire world." Uncle Tom sounded as proud of it as if he were Henry Ford himself.

Two minutes later, Uncle Tom announced, "And right here at Six Mile Road, they laid the first concrete mile in the world! They finished it just before Paul was born. It went, of course, to Seven Mile Road then. That's where we will turn for my house."

Uncle Tom and Aunt Ruby and their cousins, Paul and Mildred, lived a mile east of Woodward. Paul already turned thirteen that year. Mildred was a year older than Juanita.

"Well, here's my castle," Uncle Tom announced. "Soon I'll be planting my garden."

Uncle Tom heard Dick's groan of disbelief.

"Sooner than you think, Dick. This is a late snow, even for Michigan."

5. The Big City by Day

That Sunday, Uncle Tom strapped a big basket to the running board of his Model T. Aunt Ruby and Mom had filled it with sandwiches, pickles, lemonade and a cake.

The mild, sunny weather made it hard to believe that it snowed only a few nights before.

After they all squeezed into the car, Uncle Tom began to play tour guide again.

"Ladies and gentlemen, this is Woodward Avenue in the daylight. The man who planned the street system made it like spokes of a wheel, with Woodward being the middle spoke, and all of them starting from downtown and the Detroit River. The spokes go out to Ann Arbor, Lansing, which you know is the capital, Pontiac and Mount Clemens."

"Is there a mountain near here?" asked Walt, looking around to see out all the windows. "It's not even as hilly as Missouri. How can there be a mountain?"

"Well, someday we'll just have to go climb Mount Clemens, won't we?" Dad and Uncle Tom laughed.

"It's barely a hill," their cousin Paul explained. "Even from the river it's built along, the most they should have called it was *Mound* Clemens."

"And now, you can get a better look at where your Dad and I work. Henry Ford wanted his men to have lots of light and air, so he had it built with thousands of windows. Every window is cleaned inside and outside every week."

"The floors and machines are spotless and greaseless, too," Dad added. "It's very hard work, but not so bad when you have good air inside to breath and no slippery floors to break a leg on."

"And good pay, don't forget. Thousands of us men filled Woodward right up to the fronts of the buildings that January that Henry Ford told the newspapers he was going to pay five dollars a day. Most men weren't making half that."

"I remember when you wrote about how the police used fire hoses to keep all those men from pushing down the gates. I hope no one died of pneumonia." Mom shuddered as if she were thinking again of water being sprayed on a body in the freezing cold.

"Over there is the bank. On this next corner is the Ford Commissary, where we can buy meat and shoes at very reasonable prices. Henry Ford started that when he found out that every time he gave us a raise, the merchants raised their prices and we weren't getting the benefit of the reward for our labors."

Dad had written them that his job was working on the production line. Parts were delivered right to where the men put them on the car engine as it was rolling by on the conveyor belt. The men didn't have to move from where they were standing to get anything. The line was timed so they could do the job without rushing while it kept steadily moving.

"You've got a hard job, Herman. I was luckier. I was a machinist first at the plant on Piquette Street, before everything was moved here. Then I was an assembler for just a short while. And now I'm an inspector. It's not hard physical work but we can't let anything less than perfect pass us by.

"And down there are the big houses of the richest men in Detroit," Uncle Tom continued his narration. "Henry Ford himself used to live on that street before he built his mansion in Dearborn. See? Edison Avenue. Even Dickie should know who that's named for."

"I do," Dick sat up straight and leaned forward. "The man who invented electric lights."

"See that big squat building. It's the General Motors Building." Uncle Tom whispered the words "General Motors."

"General Motors makes cars, too." Paul also whispered. "That's a competitor company."

"Anyway, that building was finished just last year," Uncle Tom said. "It's set up like two H's connected by a line. I was told it was so every office could have its own window."

Herb counted. The General Motors Building was fifteen stories high. It covered the entire block on both of the sides they could see as they rode by.

A few minutes later, Paul pointed to their right. "Can you believe that whole building is the library? Dad says it was designed to look like something out of ancient Greece."

It was a massive structure of white stone with columns. The names of famous people were carved along the upper edge.

Uncle Tom pointed to his left. "You'll see many grand churches along Woodward Avenue. And a synagogue, too.

"The city has grown by leaps and bounds. After they took the census in 1920, they found that the population of Detroit doubled in the last ten years. And I'll bet it will double again by the next census. All due to Henry Ford paying a living wage."

The church he was pointing at was so huge and gray that it would have looked cold but for the beautiful stained glass windows. The rusty red stone of the church in the next block made it look warm and inviting.

They stopped for a signal light. This one was electric and there was no policeman in sight operating it.

"A Detroit policeman invented the first one of these lights about three years ago," Uncle Tom said. "Police officers risked getting blown up with the gas ones. You'll appreciate this, Herman. He got the idea from railroad signal lights. It took the city only a year to put up fifteen of them all over town."

Herb started seeing taller buildings and lots of them. And a lot more of the shorter ones, too. Billboards spread their legs out on the lower rooftops and advertisements decorated the entire sides of many of the tallest buildings. This was obviously downtown.

Electric lines crisscrossed above and rails shadowed below them just like the spokes of a wheel that Uncle Tom told them about. The automobiles and horse-drawn carriages had to dodge the streetcars and interurban cars. To be a pedestrian looked dangerous.

Herb got his first glimpse of the Detroit River as Uncle Tom turned left from Woodward Avenue onto Jefferson Avenue. The Mississippi River was much wider but this one was just as clear and sparkling.

"Which of you boys is best at geography? Not you, Paul, you know this one." Uncle Tom turned to look at his three nephews. Walt and Dick pointed at Herb.

"Herb? Going straight south from Detroit, what is the next foreign country you'd come to?" Uncle Tom asked.

Herb thought hard. His mind traveled down through Ohio, Kentucky, Tennessee, Georgia and Florida. "Cuba?"

"No!" Uncle Tom roared.

Dad laughed with him. "He caught me on that one, too, son."

"That I did. It's Canada! The river curves to the west for a bit so that a part of Windsor, Canada is straight south of Detroit."

They followed the river north for several miles.

"Well, here we are," Uncle Tom said. "Looks like the new Belle Isle Bridge will be finished soon. The one we're on was supposed to be temporary. The old one burned down a few years after we moved here."

"Do you see that huge stove up there? The Garland Company built it for the Chicago Exposition. We know about Expositions, don't we, Clara?" Her brother grinned at her. "Detroit was known for stove making long before the automobile makers came along."

Uncle Tom drove across the bridge to the island park and up its Central Avenue.

"They say the General there named his horse Plug Ugly, but the sign on the statue only gives his name, not his horse's."

There was a smaller statue—Newsboy and His Dog—with a drinking fountain at its base. Children raced up and down the avenue on their bicycles and rode them in circles around the statues.

Off Central Avenue was the Conservatory with domed walls of glass.

"With all those plants in there, all Paul remembers is the banana tree," his father said.

"Maybe there are orchids in there, Mom," Herb said.

"I like the Aquarium better," Paul said. "It has all kinds of fish: big ones and little ones, and all different colors, from all over the world."

The Aquarium was a round stone building with huge tanks in the center and around the curved walls.

"It's cool in here," Walt said. "I can't believe Detroit is as warm as Missouri, especially after that snow. I thought it was supposed to be much colder up North all the time."

"It amazed me, too, when I first came here," Uncle Tom said. "It's nearly the same temperatures as Missouri. Just a few degrees cooler summer and winter. We don't usually get any snow past the first week of April. But you'll have enough cold—and much more snow—soon enough," Uncle Tom warned.

"Aw, you know we get snow in Missouri," Walt said. "We have lots of snowball fights. And we build snow forts."

"By the time you finish shoveling what we get here in Michigan, you won't want to pick up any more of it, not even for a snowball fight." Uncle Tom stopped at the edge of the road alongside a spot with several picnic tables.

"I'm afraid my boys always have energy to spare," Dad said. "I'm sure Clara must have told you that many times in her letters."

After their picnic lunch, Dad rented a canoe for the boys to paddle up the canals. Juanita and Mildred rode on the pony cart. Mom looked very pleased simply to visit with Uncle Tom.

6. The New House in the Country

"Next Sunday, we'll all go see the new house," Dad said.

"*A-w-a-y* out in the country." As Aunt Ruby said this, she stretched out one arm in a grand sweep of the air.

"It's less than three miles away, Ruby," Uncle Tom admonished her.

"It's still almost all farm land. There are just a couple of houses here and there," she countered.

"You mean we won't be living in the big city?" Walt asked. "Maybe I can still go hunting. Do you have rabbits here in Michigan?"

"You mean you haven't seen the ones that try to eat my seedlings? Michigan has pretty much the same wild animals as Missouri does."

"Many of the married men at the plant are buying new houses around Ferndale," Dad said. "The village is about the same size as Oronogo. It's just spread out more and growing fast, just like Detroit. You children will still have lots of room to play and other children to play with. And Mom can still have a big garden for you to help her with."

The boys knew better than to groan out loud but Dick grunted, then quickly covered it up with a fake cough.

"The mortgage payment isn't much higher than the $6 a month rent we paid in Oronogo, especially for all we get and to own it, too," Dad continued. "Wait until you see it."

Woodward was simply one narrow band of pavement out here. The Interurban tracks were laid in the sand alongside it.

Aunt Ruby was right. There weren't many trees.

Herb could see some large tents as they turned off Woodward at what Uncle Tom explained would be Eight and a Half Mile Rd. if the half-miles were named.

"Just around this corner and down a bit," Dad said, inching forward in his seat as if to look around the corner before the car made the turn.

A sign as big as the side of a railroad car announced the Leggett Farms Subdivision.

"Is that like the Muller Subdivision in Florida, Dad?" Herb asked.

Dad liked to tell about how the truck farm they had when they lived in Florida was now known as Muller's Subdivision. "But the houses are growing up faster than the crops I tried to raise," he'd say.

"Yes, it's just like that. You can see they've taken a couple of farms and divided them up into smaller pieces for individual houses and they've already laid out streets between the rows of house lots."

"Is that the Leggett farm?" Herb pointed to a group of buildings far down the street.

"No. That farmhouse belongs to the Zinks. You can get hay for your guinea pigs there. Just remember what

28

I've told you. Don't pick one up by its tail or its eyes will fall out."

The first time Dad told them that, Juanita said, "But Daddy, guinea pigs don't have tails!"

The boys had all laughed loudly at her because they knew Dad was joking. She had begun to cry that time, so this time Dad winked at her as he said it. She smiled a little smile but Herb could tell that she still had some hurt feelings from before.

They couldn't see many houses in the subdivision, but there were sidewalks in front of where someday they would be. It still looked strange, though, to have new cement sidewalks on either side of a rutted, dusty road.

The house that was going to be theirs was *big*. Two stories high.

The real estate agent was standing on the porch.

Uncle Tom stepped out of the automobile and let the agent sit in his seat.

Mom pulled out a piece of paper money from her purse and handed it to the agent.

"Here's the down payment," she said.

"Where did Mom get that?" Dick's eyes were wide. He stared at the money as it passed from Mom to the man. "I've never seen a hundred dollar bill before."

"Hush," Herb whispered. He led Dick and Walt out of the car. "Didn't you see all the neighbors come by when they heard we were moving away? They were paying back all the money Dad loaned them."

There was a saying about a person being so generous "he'd give you the shirt off his back." Well, Dad didn't quite do that. Herb was sure he would, if the situation came up where that was the help that was needed.

From outside the car, Herb saw the keys pass from the man to Mom. "I know you will enjoy your new home, Mr. and Mrs. Muller."

Dad had brought a little can of paint and a brush. He pulled it out now and began to paint the word "Muller" on the mailbox of 1311 West Marshall Street.

"Now," he said, "let's go in and see our new home."

There were two bedrooms downstairs. Upstairs was one unfinished room, but there was flooring on the front half of it. That's where the boys were going to sleep.

Mom was most pleased by the kitchen. They had city water right from the first.

And, finally, full indoor plumbing—toilet, washbasin and bathtub. Juanita looked relieved to see the bathtub in the bathroom.

From the smirk she gave Dick, she must be remembering the time Dad suggested that since Mom had two washtubs, then two of the children could take their Saturday night bath at the same time. Dick offered to take his when Juanita took hers. Because she was so young then, it didn't occur to her that they could heat only so much water on the stove at one time anyway.

"The basin is so pretty," Juanita almost whispered.

"No more breaking the ice in the water pitcher in the mornings," crowed Dick.

"But sometimes it took ice water to wake you up," Mom said.

Walt half-closed his eyes and shuffled his feet in a circle in imitation of Dick in the morning.

"Our bathtub has clawed feet, too," Herb stooped down to examine them, "just like Uncle Tom's." Each stumpy leg ended with a ball with three thick claws around it.

The house in Oronogo didn't even have its own storm cellar but this house had a full basement. Herb figured the furnace standing in the middle of it was about three and a half feet in diameter. It had as many arms as an octopus but each of these ducts was bigger around than an elephant's leg. In its middle was a door with a wire handle.

Dad showed them the coal bin and the window where the coal would slide down a chute into their basement. He told them this was called a gravity furnace because gravity pulled down the heavier cold air through vents, the coal fire heated the air, and then the warm air rose through the ducts to heat registers in the first and the second floors.

"At first, only Herb and I will be allowed to open the door to the furnace to shovel in the coal," Dad instructed. "But Walt and Dick, you'll be allowed to shovel the ashes into a barrel to be put out into the alley every week."

Walt and Dick groaned in unison. "We always get the lousy jobs."

Their new house had electricity. They noticed how much brighter the electric lamp at Uncle Tom's was and hoped that meant they would hear more chapters each night of the Zane Grey western novel Mom had just begun reading to them.

Back outside, Herb eyed the electric pole. Mentally, he strung an antenna wire from it to the second story of the house. Carl Myers promised he'd help him make a crystal radio. Herb brought a rock of galena crystal from Oronogo for it. They'd place the galena in a piece of soft metal inside an oatmeal box cut in half and then coil the "cat whisker" wire around the upper part of the uncovered box.

"I can put my antenna wire up very high on this house. Maybe I'll be able to hear more stations. And from farther away." There were some good things about the move to Michigan after all.

However, they wouldn't have a phone. Not even a party line. The telephone cables hadn't been strung out to Leggett Farms yet. If someone needed to get an important message to the Mullers, it would have to be telegraphed to the Western Union office in Royal Oak, the next town north, and a boy would ride a bicycle to bring it to them.

"We can have our furniture delivered now," Dad said. It stayed on the train until the train reached the Royal Oak depot, where it was put into storage. Dad gave their house key to the Crydermans next door to let in the moving company. Dad also gave Mr. Cryderman the money for the storage and delivery bill.

"I'm glad to have a minister next door to us. I can worry less now, knowing that we have new neighbors we can trust," Mom declared. Dad winked at Herb. They hadn't yet seen the day that Mom worried less about anything.

"Clara, a man at work has a terrier to give away. It belonged to a neighbor of his who died so he took it in until he could find it a good home. The dog's name is Teddy. He can help protect you, too."

The four children all looked at each other, shining eyes mirroring shining eyes.

A dog!

7. Churches and Chicken Coops

They repacked their suitcases and Uncle Tom drove them to Ferndale on Sunday after church.

Mom hugged her brother. "Thank you, Tom, for everything."

"Good luck." Uncle Tom stepped up into his car and waved as he drove away.

"I'll be working the afternoon shift the next two weeks," Dad said. "We can get a lot done before I have to go to work tomorrow afternoon."

Dad and the boys placed the biggest items where Mom wanted them. Dad carefully stacked the four sections of the bookcase in the living room. He put the section without glass in its door at the bottom so it was harder to notice that it was different.

Herb looked sideways at Walt, who swallowed as he hung his head and glanced towards Dad, then quickly glanced back and glared at Herb. Herb winced. A couple years ago, Herb was looking through the family photograph album and pointed at a page.

"Here's one of you, Walt. A bare-naked-baby picture," he teased.

Walt had leaped out of the rocking chair with such force that the back of it arched like a rearing horse and slammed into the bookcase, shattering the glass on the top shelf. It took Herb a long time to pick out each splinter of glass out of all the books on that shelf. Herb figured he'd done his penance already.

"What's that smell?" Dick asked when Dad was out of the room for a moment. Sniffing like a bloodhound on the trail, he tracked it to Mom's sewing machine. He squeezed his nostrils shut with two fingers of one hand and cautiously lifted up the lid with the other hand.

They all peeked in.

"It's an assidity bag," whispered Juanita, as she backed away.

"Asafetida," Herb corrected her. He backed away too.

"Let's throw it out before Mom sees it," Dick said. Walt dashed to open the front door for Dick, who still held his nose with one hand while holding the bag in the other at the end of his fully extended arm.

Mom hung asafetida bags around their necks in winter to keep away illnesses. It also kept away anybody they could catch anything from. The bag smelled like garlic but much worse. Asafetida grew all over in Missouri. So far, they didn't see any in the fields around Uncle Tom's or West Marshall Street.

Mid-morning, Dad had set up the play tent, and Juanita was already playing house with Dale from next door. Besides the Cryderman house and theirs, there were only two other houses plus a large tent on the long block, but there were children in all of them.

Monday afternoon, Dad walked the mile to take the Interurban back down Woodward to go to work.

34

Dad asked the boys to walk with him, at least that first time, probably to give Mom a chance to get acquainted with her new home in peace and quiet.

Just like the one from Oronogo to Webb City, the Interurban was an electric rail car. Thick wires stretched above the street and a long pole on top of the car slid along one of the cables and conducted the electricity that propelled the car on the tracks.

"I can see why this is called Ferndale, Dad," Herb said. It was one huge swamp with lots of ferns growing around the edges.

"Look at those gardens." Walt pointed. "Ferns are popping up in every row. They must grow fast, 'cause it looks like those people do weed their gardens."

Scattered ferns leaned over the vegetables and flowers. Where there wasn't swamp, there was sand. And sand burs.

As the boys turned to go back home, Dad touched Herb's arm. Herb stopped while Walt and Dick started to go back.

"With this alternating shift arrangement, there'll be too many days and afternoons I won't be around. Keep an eye on things, will you, Herb?" Dad looked into Herb's eyes with the question.

"I can do that, Dad. I did get some practice this past spring, you know." Herb stood straighter and grinned as confidently as he could to reassure Dad.

Dad brought Teddy home that night. Teddy soon decided that he was Mom's protector. She couldn't go to the store without him; he followed no matter how many times she'd stop to tell him to go home.

One day that week Herb was teasing Mom and tapped her on the arm in mock roughhousing. Teddy attacked. He grabbed Herb's shirt and wouldn't let go. A piece tore off when Herb pulled away and fled outdoors. After that, Herb didn't dare to give his mother a hug if Teddy were within sight.

On the next Sunday morning, the family walked the mile to Woodward to church. The First Methodist Church was just a year old as a congregation. Herb read the letter for newcomers that was given to Dad.

Members of the Methodist Church in Royal Oak had gone door-to-door in Ferndale and found enough interest to start a church. The First Methodist Church in downtown Detroit donated $23,000. A large part of that money came from Sebastian Kresge, the man who started the S. S. Kresge Five-and-Dime stores.

Construction was already started on three lots on the west side of Woodward but for now, services and Sunday School classes were being held in the Oddfellows Hall.

"Odd fellows!" Walt exclaimed.

"Odd fellows?" Dick echoed

Herb shrugged.

The Hall commanded the whole second floor above a shop on the east side of Woodward.

"Good morning, folks. I'm Archie T. Taylor. We know it's a little crowded now in the lodge here," Mr. Taylor greeted them. "At least this is more comfortable than what the Catholics first used. The lone structure left on the lots they bought was a chicken coop, so on Sunday mornings you'd see folks on their knees outside the coop waiting their turn for communion."

After his sermon at the makeshift pulpit, the Reverend John Dystant made an announcement.

"Mr. Taylor of the Building Committee informs me that construction is proceeding according to schedule for the first phase of our building plan. We should be able to look forward to the dedication of the social hall, the Sunday School rooms and the gym shortly after the first of the new year."

Mr. Taylor came up to them after the service.

"Hello again, little lady." He bent down and smiled at Juanita.

"Did you meet my granddaughter, Betty, this morning? You look to be about her age."

"Go ahead, Girlie. Answer him," Dad said. He grinned at Mr. Taylor. "Cat must have got her tongue again. I keep telling the boys to keep that cat fed so it doesn't go after Juanita."

"Yes, sir, I did." Juanita said half of that as she slid behind Mom and clutched her skirt.

"This is my wife, Emma. I own the A. T. Taylor Shoe Store up north of the Nine Mile Road. I'd be glad to have you stop by the store, even if you don't need shoes. And bring Juanita. She and Betty can play together."

Reverend Dystant approached. "Mr. Taylor is one of our church's charter members. He's also a member of the Oddfellows Lodge and arranged our services to be here."

"Mr. Taylor, sir." Walt saw his opportunity. "Why did he say you are an odd fellow? I don't see anything odd about you. There's supposed to be a whole bunch of you odd fellows who meet here?"

Mom blushed and reached for Walt's collar. The men all laughed.

"No, young man. Oddfellows is an organization that started in England about 200 years ago. There are two stories about why it was called Oddfellows. Back then, there were several groups of skilled tradesmen, like the brick masons and carpenters, who came together for socializing and helping each other, so it could have been because it was a group of those without a group.

"The other story is that it was made up of ordinary workingmen who were not in the skilled trades and for them to gather together was thought rather odd. Either way, it was looked upon as a group of odd fellows. So here we are."

8. Cross Fires

There was a lot of open space, just as Dad promised. There were no other houses between their street and the Eight Mile Road. A field stretched behind the house with a lone walnut sentinel. Thick woods edged the field, surrounding a swamp so large that the center of it looked more like a weedy lake.

It was very quiet. On cool nights they could hear boat whistles on the Detroit River eleven miles away.

Walt and Dick chased snakes and rabbits in the fields. Sometimes they actually caught rabbits.

"All you have to know," Herb heard Walt tell their new friend Jack, "is that they run in circles. I run in one direction around the circle —"

"And I run in the other direction —" Dick added.

"And when it gets tired, we catch it." Walt finished.

"And when *you* catch one, we'll call it a Jack's rabbit," Dick said. They all laughed.

Florence LaPointe lived down the street in the large army tent while her father and brothers built their new home. She often invited Juanita over to play house.

"Florence makes us mustard sandwiches," Juanita told her brothers.

"Mustard sandwiches?" Dick made a sour face.

"They're very good," Juanita insisted.

The boys' favorite climbing trees each had a branch just low enough for the boys to pull themselves up on but too high for Juanita. She'd run crying to Mom or to Mrs. Cryderman that first summer.

Herb often took Juanita into the field to pick chokeberries and wildflowers. On one of these walks, he found a long snakeskin.

"Here's a fur stole for you, Nita," he said as he draped it around her neck.

"Get that snake off me!" she shrieked. She slid out from under it and darted up to the house. "Mommy! Mommy!"

To the west of them, towards the village of Oak Park, bog fires erupted here and there and smoldered for weeks, producing a continuous dark smoke that sometimes reached their house.

The fire in the field on the corner west of them one night wasn't the bog burning. Someone made a wooden cross, stood it up and set it on fire.

"It's a good thing the ground is so sandy here," Dad said. "It will keep the fire from spreading."

Then he said, so low Herb could barely hear him, "It looks too much like the work of the KKK." Dad's face squeezed into a puzzled expression before he shook his head as if to shake that idea out of it.

Herb knew about the Ku Klux Klan and the crosses they were known for planting and lighting. And the white costumes they wore with masks to hide the faces of the men who were deciding the fate of people without bothering with a judge much less a jury.

When the rest of the family came back into the house after the fire was doused, Herb found Juanita awake. She was lying on Mom and Dad's bed, solemnly staring out the window at the smoldering wood.

The next night, Herb sat at the table until late with his crystal radio set. He wanted to see how far away he could get stations. Cincinnati was the farthest so far. So he wouldn't wake his brothers, he slept in the living room.

Crash!

It sounded like it came from the back of the house. Mom heard it, too. Herb saw her standing in her bedroom doorway. Then they heard crackling sounds. And smelled wood burning. He stood up.

"Herm, there's a fire at the back of the house!" Mom screamed. She saw Herb in the living room.

"Get Juanita. I'll get the boys."

Mom dashed upstairs for Walt and Dick. Teddy yipped at Mom's heels as she dashed back down the stairs and wheeled around into the bathroom.

"The back wall is on fire!" she screamed as she filled a pail with water from the bathtub faucet.

Dad found the fire on their back porch. He grabbed the hose from the side of the house and Mr. Cryderman, who had leaped out of his bed at the commotion, now aimed his hose at the fire from the other side. Soon the flames turned into a mere whining sizzle.

Mom and her brood huddled together and not because they were cold. It was a warm night even without flames.

"The back door fell in onto the kitchen floor," Dad said, as he was regaining his breath.

"But what caught fire?" Mom asked.

"It looks like a fire was set under the porch and it spread," Dad said.

"But who? Why?" Mom began to shake and wrapped her arms tighter around herself.

"I couldn't begin to guess that. We haven't been here long enough to have enemies," Dad frowned and shook his head.

Mom fixed her eyes on Walt. "Who have you been fighting with?" Walt was not a bully but he did like a good scrap now and then.

"No one, Mom, honest." Walt was shaking, too.

They all were. Juanita still clung to Herb. He hadn't put her down since he'd pulled her out of her bed.

"Daddy," she said in a tiny voice. Herb handed her to Dad.

"You know, boys, how I always tell you to put away tools when you are done with them?" Dad grinned slightly. "And to do as I say not as I do?" He looked around at them. "It was a good thing tonight that I didn't do as I say. I'm glad I'd left the hose still hooked up to the house."

Their neighbor frowned when he saw the full extent of the damage. "There's a group of KKK a few miles over who don't want Southerners up here, colored or white," he said. "They claim to be doing God's work. I don't call that Christian."

The Ferndale police came by the next day. They studied the footprints. One measured out to be thirteen inches long.

"That must have been a large man," the officer remarked to his fellow policeman.

Juanita squeezed Herb's hand tighter as they watched the police do their investigation.

Later, one of the officers came back to report that they'd been able to follow the prints all the way to Eight Mile Road but lost them once the suspects went onto the pavement.

Reverend Cryderman was also a carpenter. Actually, he looked more like a carpenter than like a minister. He was taller than Dad, who wasn't short as it was, and thicker, probably most of it muscle. He rebuilt the porch for them.

Afterwards, he took one of the studs and called his son and the Muller boys over to the space between their houses.

"Did you boys know that a two by four isn't? It's not quite two inches by four inches. I don't know why it's that way; it goes back probably centuries." He grinned. "Maybe the king's thumb was smaller then. You know that's how the English came up with the inch. The king measured the width of an average man's thumb."

Mr. Cryderman laid the two-by-fours that weren't two by four on the ground parallel to each other and four feet apart.

"Dale, go get the two wooden boxes in our basement that are about 18 inches by 24 inches. Dick and Walt, go with him. Dick, you bring back the four broom handles and Walt can get the old roller skates by them. Herb, your mother saved four tin cans for us."

When they returned, they saw Mr. Cryderman cutting the six-foot stud into two pieces. Then he picked up his hammer and a box of nails. All four boys stared at the pile of materials, puzzled.

"First, we nail one set of the rollers at each end of our two-by-fours." Each boy nailed one set on. "Then we lay the studs down on the wheels and center the box on the stud at one end so the tall side of the box is standing up."

The boys went from being mystified to becoming excited. Scooters!

"Nail the box down the middle onto the stud." Mr. Cryderman handed the hammer to Walt. "Careful now, we want it to be secure.

"Now, Carl, nail down the broom handles to the edges of the boxes. They must be nailed down tight, too. Here's a trick. Pound the nail almost through the broomstick before you place it onto the box."

Herb was waiting to nail the tin cans on the front to look like headlamps. They'd seen boys put candles in the cans and light them so that at night they looked almost like those on a car.

Within the week, the parents ordered the boys to use their scooters on the sidewalk on the opposite side of the street so Juanita and her friends could play hopscotch and "Mother May I" without being run over.

Dad, however, wasn't even a good handyman. After the first heavy rain, the front door swelled up and would not close tightly, so Dad planed the bottom of the door. After that, the wind squeezed through between the door and the doorsill where Dad had scraped it down too much. Herb remembered that Mom was the one who nailed tin can lids onto the floor to keep the rats from crawling through the knotholes at the shack where they first lived in Oronogo. She was handier with a hammer than Dad.

It was a very hot summer. Mom decided to read *The Call of the Wild*, by Jack London, to them. Just like James Oliver Curwood's books, it helped them feel frozen tundra around them rather than steaming sand.

9. New Schools

The first time Mom sent Herb by himself to Sabaugh's corner store, Sam Sabaugh asked him if he'd like to deliver groceries for him.

"I would like that very much," Herb said quickly. "Back in Missouri, I delivered papers, so I already have experience delivering things."

"Would you be able to start right away? You'll earn $5 a week plus whatever tips you get. That'll buy a lot of things a young man might want."

Herb heard Juanita moaning in bed one morning as he left for his job. He looked at Mom, with his own worried expression.

"Her ears have gathered again. You know how much that hurts but I've given her some medicine to take away at least a bit of the pain from the infection."

Juanita didn't seem to be feeling much better when Herb came back from delivering groceries for Sam. That is, until he gave her the box of Cracker Jack he bought for her from a tip a customer gave him.

That July, the family celebrated Herb's thirteenth birthday in the new house. Mom always made angel food cake for birthdays. She instructed Herb to sift the flour exactly thirteen times.

Mom's cook stove here used kerosene. Herb remembered how good it had smelled when oak wood was used in the one back home in Missouri but the angel food cake still tasted good here in Michigan.

After supper, they all sang "Happy Birthday."

Herb smiled and dutifully bent over for Dad to give him the thirteen birthday swats "and one to grow on."

Herb started eighth grade at the Abraham Lincoln High School that fall. Being a new student didn't feel at all as uncomfortable as Herb remembered feeling when he was five they had just moved to Oronogo. Likely it was because more kids here were new than not.

There were also many more students here than there had been in Missouri. In fact, there were so many families moving in and houses filling in the vacant lots that the school, although three stories tall and barely three years old, already needed new additions. There were temporary wooden structures and for a month Herb attended class in one of these annexes.

A few of the other new students spoke with accents. Some of them sounded somewhat like Grandmother Muller's German and some a bit more like Grandmother Sincox's English. Others sounded very different from either. There were a few colored students, who lived in a section around the Nine and Half Mile Road east of Woodward. None of them had Southern accents, as Herb expected.

The school was on Rockwell Avenue that went east and west from Woodward "on the Nine Mile." To get to school, Herb walked up Pinecrest Road, which became Ridge Road at Rockwell. The land did sit higher there.

Opposite the school at the corner of Farmdale was Croton's Sweet Shoppe, with its ice cream parlor and candy counter. Students bought delicious hot dogs with relish and mustard for lunch. Mrs. Croton treated them as if they were her own children.

Walter, Dick and Juanita went to Washington School, which was new as of that spring.

"I get hand-me-downs just because I'm adopted." Dick complained.

Walt rolled his eyes. He and Herb knew Dick was born into the family but Juanita fell for it.

"But you look like Daddy," she pointed out.

"Except for that nose," Walt added.

"You're lucky, Nita," Dick ignored that last remark. "You don't get hand-me-downs."

"Who's she going to get them from, Mom?" asked Walt.

"Stop grousing, Richard," Mom said.

Dick groused about school, too.

"At Washington, the teachers are so-o-o strict. You can't talk out loud at all or chew gum. We have to know the times tables and they keep on having spelling bees. And Teacher won't let me write my full name on my papers."

"He means all those names that he says are his," Juanita informed Mom.

"That's right. Richard Lee Jackson Samuel Emanuel Muller. 'Cause I'm adopted. Which were my names before I was adopted, Mom?"

"Richard," Mom began. "Are you trying the patience of your teachers like you try mine?"

After one rainstorm, Mom surprised them all by putting on a pair of Walt's pants and leading them in wading barefoot in the puddles made by the ruts in the road. However, those same ruts trapped wheels like quicksand. Or "quickmud" as Dick called it.

A wagon could get stuck up to its axles. Wagons powered by horses could be pulled out. Those with engines had to be pushed, or someone with a horse could help pull it out, but not without remarks like, "Get a horse!"

If Walt's body had axles, he would have managed to get up to them in mud, too. One afternoon, Mom told him to stay out on the porch until he cleaned off his shoes. Instead, he simply took them off and came into the house in his stocking feet.

"Walter, I told you to clean the mud off your shoes."

"Why? They'll just get all muddy again tomorrow."

"You do as I say." Mom's pointer finger cut the air near Walt's ear.

Walt ducked and ran. Mom ran after him. He scooted into their parent's bedroom and slid under their big bed. Mom tried to grab him. He rolled back and forth, just out of her reach.

"You wait until your father comes home," she warned him as she got up from the floor.

Dad was working midnights that week. They were eating breakfast when he came home. He was barely through the door.

"Daddydon'thitme," Walt cried out.

Dad looked at Mom, whose chin pulled her head down in a firm nod.

Dad sighed. He signaled for Walt to follow him.

Walt walked slowly, with his head down, but Herb saw him sneak a sideways grin at Dick. Herb and Dick looked at each other. They knew full well that Dad wouldn't hit Walt.

Just as he did now, Dad would take the condemned boy into his parents' bedroom and close the door. They heard him say, "Bend over," but they knew he followed that with a whisper, "Yell real loud."

Outside that door, you'd hear ten hard slaps and ten loud yells. Behind the door, the boys knew Dad was slapping his right hand down hard on his own left hand those ten times.

The scolding that went along with it was real, though. Especially the part about not giving Mom such a hard time. Juanita never got the "spankings." With just a look from Mom, Juanita began weeping so she rarely even got a scolding.

This morning, however, the last yell from Walt sounded different than the other nine. It was sharper, as though he was surprised. Herb noticed that Dad was joking less lately after a long day at the factory.

10. Holidays

The days began to cool. Mom asked Mr. Krause to start delivering coal so they could fill the bin well before the first frost.

Dad was home for one of those deliveries. Mom had gone to a meeting of the ladies at the church.

Dad took Mr. Krause aside for a moment so the boys couldn't hear their conversation. Then Mr. Krause nodded his head and both men smiled at the boys.

"Walt. Dick. Come here.' Dad waved them over. "Mr. Krause is going to drive his horse very slowly so each of you can have a special ride. Put your hands on the spokes of the wheel right here, and here," Dad pointed at the top near the rim, "and put your feet on the rim. Hang on tight."

Walt and Dick were just the right height for this trick. As the wheels turned slowly, they went around like circus performers. When the wagon stopped, they got off and came back grinning as wide as if it were Christmas morning.

"Thank you, Mr. Krause," Dad shouted. Then to all three of the boys, he said, "Don't ask to do it again. *And* I know I don't need to tell you to not tell your mother."

"Oh, no. We won't," they promised.

The fun they'd had and the secret they were keeping was almost too much. When Mom returned, their fidgety grins and eager offers to help her carry in her bags led to a suspicious expression on her face. She looked at Dad.

"Oh, I've promised to take the boys to see where we might find a Christmas tree for next month. You know how helpful they get when they remember Christmas is coming."

Mom wasn't convinced but she closed the discussion with one of her "there'd better not be any trouble" looks and followed her helpers into the house.

For Halloween, a neighbor farther down their street decorated the outside of his house to be scary. But inside he had pulled out his dining table to full length, put in all its leaves, and covered every square inch with different kinds of candy — jawbreakers, candy corn and jelly beans in little bags, Barnum's Animal Crackers, Peppermint Life Savers, Good and Plenty, Tootsie Rolls, Mary Janes, Necco Wafers, Hershey's Kisses, Chuckles, the coconut Konabar, and chocolate-covered candy bars: Baby Ruth, Mounds, Milky Way and Clark bars.

"He must be rich," Dick said, his eyes wide.

Herb knew Dick's stomach was much bigger than his eyes. He never could understand how Dick could eat so much sweet stuff and not get sick. Herb's stomach had punished him for eating too many cherries from the tree in front of their house in Oronogo. He wasn't going to risk a repeat from too much sweet candy.

"Help yourselves, boys and girls," their host said. "And for the mothers, I have chocolate covered cherries and a Whitman's Sampler to select from."

The neighbor enjoyed the company. He encouraged the children to fill their bags and talked with them about fun things, not about school like other adults always asked.

When Thanksgiving came, Uncle Tom picked them up for dinner at his house with turkey and all the trimmings.

"You all moved out of my house just in time. Mildred came down with scarlet fever, the house was quarantined and they sealed off Mildred's room for six weeks."

"Your Uncle Tom had to climb in and out of the window to go to work," Aunt Ruby said. "After they lifted the quarantine, I had to boil everything she touched that I could boil and clean everything else with a strong chemical. But we're glad she's fine now."

Mildred looked fine and she could see fine, too. Herb knew that once in a while a child's eyes were affected by scarlet fever, and some even went blind.

Christmas in Ferndale was a village celebration, too. In front of Central School, which was on the corner of Woodward and the Nine Mile, was a small park with big trees and benches. One of the evergreen trees was decorated with electric lights. Someone put an evergreen bough on the Crow's Nest, the tower where the police officer stood to direct traffic on that busy intersection.

At the appointed time, with hundreds gathered around, the switch was thrown and the lights on the tree all came on at once. The high school glee clubs led the singing of the Christmas carols.

At home, their tree wore a long necklace of electric lights, draped around several times. Last Christmas,

51

without electricity, Dad had put candles on their tree. He gathered the family around and quickly lit the candles. They took it all in with a deep breath and then blew out the candles before a fire could start.

At the Christmas Eve service at church all the children were given little boxes of penny candies.

"Juanita, I'll trade my gumdrops for your jawbreakers," Dick offered.

"And a Mary Jane," Juanita counter offered.

"Awww, that's a hard bargain," Dick paused as if he were considering it. Herb and Walt knew it was just an act that didn't convince anyone. "But alright."

"Here's another Mary Jane for you," Walt said. "Already wrapped for your Christmas present."

Uncle Otto sent them a check, as he did each Christmas. Herb once heard Uncle Otto explain that with only one child and a good job at the railroad, he was able to be Santa's helper and it gave him much pleasure to do that.

Dick gave Herb an erector set. Herb wanted one so he could build his own skyscraper. The flat metal pieces would be scale-model beams in his tower.

He bought tinker toys for Dick.

"So he can make something besides trouble," Mom suggested.

Dick put one of the round pieces onto one of the dowels and pretended it was a hammer. He looked over at Juanita.

Juanita ran to Dad.

Mom and Dad gave Juanita a beautiful doll with hair coming out of her head just like real hair. Juanita named her doll Rose Marie.

The children gave Mom a box of candy.

"Oh, if only I could have three sweet boys," Mom said, "I'd give up chocolates."

They all knew that she'd never get the one, nor give up the other.

Then Dad picked up his guitar and they sang Christmas songs together. Dad let Juanita, who had the best voice of them all, pick the songs and start them. She'd learned a new one this year and sang out at the top of her voice:

"It Came Upon A Midnight Shift..." They all burst out laughing, leaving Juanita perplexed and not knowing whether to laugh or to cry.

For New Year's Eve, Uncle Tom's family visited them. This year his Model T must have decided it was too cold to travel. So Mom wouldn't worry when they didn't arrive, they took the Interurban streetcar, got off at Marshall Street and then walked the frigid mile to the house. Aunt Ruby tried to smile but Herb still heard the word "country" escape between her chattering teeth. At least there was the shanty at the Interurban stop to give them some shelter from the cold while they waited for the ride home.

Each year one more of them was able to make it to midnight to say, "Happy New Year" before dragging off to bed. This year would have been Dick's turn but he'd eaten too much as usual, which made him sleepy.

That January, the church dedicated the large gym and the social hall. Services were held in the social hall, and the gym was partitioned off with makeshift "walls" for Sunday School classes.

Reverend Dystant was a charter member of the Royal Oak Rotary Club and announced that it was planning an organization meeting in order to set one up in Ferndale. It would have its first meeting at the Oddfellows Hall.

Although it snowed quite a bit in the hills of Missouri, the winters were longer here. The postman counted on the warm cup of coffee at the Mullers, halfway through his route. This time of year, a window box outside the kitchen served as an icebox for the cream.

Mom started reading to them earlier in the evenings. The Zane Grey westerns made it seem warmer than it was. Walt wanted the next book to be anything by James Oliver Curwood. *Isobel, A Romance of the Northern Trail*, was Walt's favorite so far.

"With all this snow, you want a book about Canada?" Dick asked.

"Don't forget, Dick, it's a romance, too," Herb teased.

"That's what I can't understand" Mom shook her head. "How a boy who likes to fight so much always wants me to read love stories."

"Adventure *and* love stories," Walt defended himself. Or tried to. "I was only thinking of how a book needs to have adventure for us boys and a love story for you and Nita."

But they'd all seen him show off whenever girls his age were around. Even on ice skates.

Ice skating was something nearly everyone did. There were two rinks at the state fairgrounds at the Eight Mile Road and Woodward, and also two that Henry Ford had built in Highland Park south of the Six Mile Road. At each location, while one rink was being used by the skaters, the other had been reflooded and was freezing to make a smooth surface again.

There were warming rooms and those who had money could buy hot dogs and hot chocolate. The Mullers usually brought something to eat.

Because Paul and Mildred lived about midway between the fairgrounds and Highland Park, they saw their cousins more often now, at one rink or the other.

Walt and Dick still caught rabbits. When the snow was deep, they took a cardboard box out with them. They found a rabbit tunnel and put the box at the opening. While one held onto the box, the other poked a stick into the snow until he woke up the rabbit.

"Nita," Herb heard Walt call out to their sister one Sunday afternoon. "Come see our Easter dinner."

Juanita stepped out onto the back porch and peeked into the box. She saw the scared furry creature inside it.

"That's why they call it the Easter bunny, you know," Dick teased.

"We are *not* going to have rabbit for dinner," Juanita shrieked. "*You let it go!*"

The boys laughed and took it out to the field.

11. Springtime

When they saw Mr. Krause again in the spring, he was delivering ice. A box on the back porch had kept food cold all winter.

In their window was a card with a number in each corner. Mr. Krause knew how much ice was wanted by whichever number — 25, 50, 75 or 100 — was in the top left corner.

With huge metal tongs, he grabbed a 25 pound chunk of ice and put it into one side of the double washtubs, which stood on tin legs in the basement, the coolest place in the house. Mom kept the butter cool by packing it around the ice and covering it with a towel. As the ice melted, one of them pulled the plug for the water to go down the basement drain.

"Tonic time," Herb called. They all smelled the sassafras tea Mom was brewing. Fortunately, it didn't smell bad, like the asafetida. "Get your spring tonic now. Guaranteed to clean out your blood from any winter poisons." Herb imitated a carnival barker well.

Spring also meant kites.

While Herb made a box kite he designed himself, Dick and Walt made the common diamond-shaped kites. They cut a yardstick down the middle lengthwise, crossed one piece with the other about a third of the way down and tied them together. Next, they tied string to all four points, pulling the crosspiece into a bow about six inches long.

A piece of newspaper was cut one inch larger than the frame all around and pasted on with a flour and water mixture from Mom's kitchen. The trickiest part was carefully folding the paper over the string to lock it in. They added a four-foot string tail with pieces of rags tied on it to swing in the breeze.

They rewound the string ball onto a stick just long enough for a hand on each side of the rolled up string. Finally, they tied the loose end of string from the string ball to the spot on the kite where the sticks crossed. It was ready to fly.

"Let me go first," Walt said. "I can run the fastest."

He sprinted down the field, holding the rolled up string in one hand and the kite by its cross strings in the other. He unrolled enough slack in the supply of string for the kite to start taking off when the wind caught it, but not so much as to make the kite nosedive into the ground.

As soon as the kite sailed upwards into the air, he stopped running and started playing out the string as fast as both hands could roll the stick. With an occasional tug, the kite responded with a bow or a dip.

At church one Sunday morning, Walt couldn't resist telling Mr. Taylor his biggest news.

"We found a dead horse in the field behind our house. It must have been dead a while, because it was already getting all bloated. And the flies — "

57

Mom was trying to change the conversation but Mr. Taylor was already responding to Walt's report.

"That reminds me of the police officer who found one near here a few years ago. He had to make a report and didn't know how to spell Breckenridge. He had the carcass pulled over to the next street. Withington is easier to spell, I'll grant you that."

Dale Cryderman was a year younger than Dick so they played together often, especially once Walt started finding places to play basketball. Dick and Dale pitched tents on the sand and played war and "the foreign legion on the desert."

Dale was the only child of Reverend and Mrs. Cryderman. Obviously, Mrs. Cryderman wished she had a girl, too. She made a dress for Juanita for a Christmas present and another for her birthday in March.

"We're so fortunate to have had such wonderful neighbors, both in Oronogo and here," Mom said on these occasions, and others, too.

"This dress is pretty, too," Juanita said. "And I still miss Miss Blanche."

The neighborliness went both ways.

Years before, Mrs. Cryderman had tuberculosis. It left her muscles weak so Herb mixed her cake batter for her. Herb liked making things, and kitchens were full of opportunities.

When Mom helped at the voting polls, Herb made sandwiches for her. She told him how the other ladies marveled that a young man could make such dainty ones and how carefully he cut off the crusts.

" 'Like a fancy chef,' " one of them said.

" 'Like future engineer, is more like it,' I told them," Mom smiled at Herb.

Whenever Mom worked at the polls, Walt walked her home after the votes were counted. The morning after the April election, Walt swaggered up to Herb, who was getting ready to leave for Sabaugh's store.

"Good morning, Herb," Walt said. "I'll have you know that you're not the only lucky one. I got a job now, too."

"You didn't have one yesterday. Did you get elected to something?" Herb asked.

"No. Seriously. When I went to get Mom last night, Mrs. Weber asked me if I'd like to work in the greenhouse with Mr. Weber. 'He needs another young man,' she said, 'who is energetic and likes to earn money.'"

Herb laughed. "You like to spend it! That's the truth of the matter. But I suspected you've got Dad's green thumb. I knew you liked working in the garden. I never believed all that grumbling you did when we had to weed."

School had been out only two weeks but Mom already left the house three times, without a word, to take a very brisk walk around the block. Alone. She wouldn't even take Teddy, so he stared out the screen door and whimpered until she returned.

As she neared their house after the third time, the neighbor from across the street called out. He walked towards their house.

"Clara?"

"Yes? How are you?"

"I'm fine, thank you. Would you mind if tomorrow after church I took your children out to Walled Lake with me for the day? I imagine they would enjoy the ride — it's a bit over 20 miles — and they could go swimming."

Herb was on the front steps, sketching the next skyscraper for his erector set. He saw Mom take a deep breath. Her shoulders dropped as she exhaled.

"That will be wonderful. I'm sure they will enjoy it very much."

And so will you, Mom. Just that morning Herb heard her mutter, "It's going to be a long summer." Right after Dick and Dale Cryderman dashed three times around the house as whooping, shooting cowboys and Indians, and Juanita asked again for more tea for herself and her dolls, and Walt slammed the back door coming in to use the toilet and slammed it again going back out to play.

Mom packed a lunch for all five of them, with the largest piece of cake for their neighbor.

"Children, you be on your best behavior." She tried to be dignified but it was easy for Herb to see the prospect of relief in her eyes. Herb would be willing to bet their kind neighbor noticed it, too, and that that was his intention, besides getting away from the scorching sandy lots himself.

12. Rolling Forward

Although Dad helped make the Ford Model T, the family wasn't any closer to getting their own Tin Lizzie. So they still walked, not just to church, but to nearly everywhere.

They walked to Sam and Irma Sabaugh's Market, which was less than half a mile away. Mom might give them a dollar to get the food she needed for supper. Or Sam let them get food "on tag" until Dad's payday.

Dick begged to go with Mom when she went shopping in downtown Ferndale.

"I can carry all your packages for you," he offered.

Herb, and Mom, knew the real reason. After the first time they stopped for lunch at the diner near the police station, Dick came back with the report that "they serve the greasiest ol' chili, but was it good!"

Mom, Juanita and Dick rode with Mrs. Cryderman in her car when she went to visit her mother one day.

"She started to turn the steering wheel and the darn thing came right off in her hands." Dick laughed.

"She shoved it right back on real fast and kept right on going."

As they neared Woodward on Sundays, they saw cars lined up tire to tire as far north and south as one could see, inching forward maybe a yard at a time. Horns honked, "Ah-oo-gah. Ah-oo-gah." Drivers leaned out the windows as if that would make the line move.

They saw the officer up in the Crow's Nest. He was obviously trying to be fair in how often he turned the signal in each direction to keep traffic flowing, but with that many cars and only one lane each way, it flowed like thick mud uphill.

"If I had to deal with that many drivers, I'd want to be twelve feet up in the air with a thick concrete base below me, too." Herb said.

"Did I tell you one of the tales I heard in the barber shop about the Crow's Nest?" Dad asked. "The village officials used to take turns operating it in the evenings. You see the ladder on the side of the pole? Well, it leads to a little door up into the nest. A very little door. The village president was, shall we say, portly. He became stuck trying to squeeze himself through. The fellows in the barber shop who knew the man were laughing so hard I couldn't find out if he ever made it in and if he did, how they got him out."

In 1924, Woodward Avenue became known as The Widest Highway in the World. It went from only 18 feet wide to 204 feet wide. The state seized the front part of their church site for the widening. In exchange, the state paid the church $35,000 for damages and loss of land. The church trustees immediately met to plan how to use this much money for building projects.

The Crow's Nest was removed for the widening. So were some of the graves in the Hebrew cemetery between Marshall and the Eight Mile Road.

Herb and others of the older children watched the process and progress for several days before getting bored with it.

Many more people had cars, though the Mullers still didn't. Some men used their cars to offer a jitney service. They put white signs behind the windshield so Mom knew, when she did her shopping on Woodward, which man was available for hire to load her purchases into his car and drive her home.

That summer, on the next corner north from their church, the Zion Lutheran Church began construction. There were now three churches in three blocks on Woodward. Ferndale was beginning to look like a city.

On a clear afternoon that fall, they heard lions roar from one and a half miles north of them in Royal Oak where the Detroit Zoo was gradually taking shape. They looked at each other in disbelief.

Uncle Tom heard them tell Paul about it when they visited later that week.

"Even though this zoo will be away out in the country," Uncle Tom winked at his wife, "I voted in favor of the taxes for Detroit to have a zoo. It's getting to be bigger than St. Louis so it should have a zoo, too. Besides, Detroit will have expanded out there by the time it's done."

Early one morning, Walt dashed into the yard. "Mr. Lash is moving his house! Let's go watch." He and Dick scurried down the street and around the corner. Herb followed at a walk.

Mr. Lash's oldest son, also named Herbert, was drinking a cup of water, a shovel in his hand.

"Why is your father moving the house?" Herb asked.

"Well, when he built it, he put it in the middle of our lot. That didn't leave room for a driveway. He wants to put a basement under it, too. So he might as well do both at the same time." Herbert went back to work.

The house was already up on skids—thick beams parallel to each other in the direction the house was to move. Herb, Walt and Dick watched Mr. Lash and men from the neighborhood as they used railroad jacks to push the house eight feet along on the skids over the big hole dug for the basement.

Seems as though he would have planned that out at the beginning. Their own house was built with the basement and space for a driveway and they still didn't have a car. When would Dad be able to get one? After all, he helped make them. Everybody knew Mr. Ford said he was trying to make cars cheap enough so ordinary people could afford them.

Once in a while, Mom had Herb bring home some malt in Sabaugh's delivery wagon. Dad used it to mix a batch of home brew in a large crock in the basement. The smell of fermenting was a warm yet strong smell. Herb knew chemical reactions often brought heat even without a flame underneath and that all cooking, baking and brewing were chemical reactions.

Herb tasted Dad's homemade beer once. He couldn't see why they needed Prohibition to keep people from drinking it. But Dad liked a mug of it, especially after work.

"Funny thing about Prohibition," Dad said. He took another swallow of beer. "The newspaper says that Detroit had 1,500 bars before it was voted in and that now it has anywhere between 5,000 and maybe even 25,000 blind pigs."

Herb knew that "blind pigs" weren't animals but rather hidden rooms where adults went to drink the forbidden alcohol.

"It's drunkenness that's the evil, not the drinking," Mom said.

13. A Baby and A Bob

Mom joined the Methodist Ladies' Aid Society. The ladies took turns hosting the meetings in their homes. When they met at the Muller's, just before dessert, Mom asked Juanita to stand on a chair to say the prayer.

"I wish she wouldn't make me do it," Juanita complained to Herb. "It feels like I'm on a stage and I don't like to do that."

"But you're used to performing. Dad always had you stand up to sing when he played his guitar at Grandmother's and Uncle Otto's."

"Only singing and only for family," she insisted.

When the Ladies Aid Society served lunch for the Rotary Club that was now meeting at their church, Mom baked biscuits. She told her family at supper that all the ladies wanted her recipe. She was pleased at the compliment.

Herb was often in the kitchen with her. He never saw her look at a recipe and was sure she never made anything quite the same way each time. Even so, her cooking always tasted delicious.

One afternoon when Dad came home from working the day shift, he stood in the doorway as usual, sniffing to guess what was for supper.

"Plenty of nothing, Dad," Walt told him. "Mom's at Etienne's. Her boys came over here yelling for her. Their mother's going to have her baby and the doctor hadn't come yet."

Reverend Cryderman's congregation built a new church a mile north of the old one so the Cryderman family had moved to be closer to it. The Etienne family now lived in the house next door.

Herb helped Dad fix some cold roast beef sandwiches. Mom came in as they were eating.

"Well, it was good that I went over there to help. The doctor arrived after I already cut the cord," Mom said as she came in the door. "Lizzy had a healthy baby girl."

Mom slumped into her chair. "Now she has two boys and two girls. She is so lucky," Mom looked fondly at Juanita.

"What are they going to name the baby?" asked Juanita.

"Betty May. Betty after her own mother. The name Lizzie comes from Elizabeth and so does Betty. And Grandmother Etienne's name is May.

"She offered to pay me, Herm. I told her that country folk don't charge others for doing such things. We didn't in Missouri and it still looks like country out here to me."

Families often did their own doctoring. "Grandma" Myers always knew which weeds were safe to eat and which ones made medicine. Her son Carl built a house for his family three blocks straight north on Leroy Street. For the first couple of years, until more homes filled in between them, they could see the front of the

Myers' house. Mom still called on Grandma Myers when one of the children came down with a new malady.

That evening, they gathered around the table and Mom began to read poems from *The Spell of the Yukon,* by Robert Service.

> *A bunch of the boys were whooping it up*
> > *in the Malamute saloon;*
> *The kid that handles the music-box was*
> > *hitting a jag-time tune;*
> *Back of the bar, in a solo game, sat*
> > *Dangerous Dan McGrew,*
> *And watching his luck was his light-o'-love,*
> > *the lady that's known as Lou.*

"When I grow up, I'm going to go see that Malamute Saloon," Dick vowed.

A popular game for boys up here in Michigan was running through the fields and then counting to find out who caught the most sand burs on his pants.

At least in the time it took them to count the hundreds of them, they were staying out of other trouble.

"You be sure to pull off every one of those stick-tights ," Mom warned. "I don't need to find them in the wash."

"Of course we pull them all off, Mom." Dick said. "That's the only way we find out who won."

Mom long ago learned to check pockets very carefully before she put the clothes into the big tub on the stove to boil.

After the clothes boiled a while, she took out the first piece of clothing, lathered the big brown bar of Fels Naptha soap all over the item and then rubbed it up and down on the metal washboard.

"She's rubbing so hard you'd think it was Walt instead of his pants on that board," Dick said to Herb.

"Couldn't be your pants. Not ever since you left those crawdads in your pockets and they rotted," Walt retorted.

After scrubbing the clothes on the washboard, Mom rinsed them in another tub of boiling water. She wrung as much of the water out of them as she could.

After she filled a basket with them, she had Walt and Dick each take a handle and carry it to the backyard. Four thin ropes were stretched between two "T" poles for clothes lines. Long wooden poles with notches in them propped up the lines with the heavier loads.

Mom's hair was so long she could almost sit on it after she took it down from the pompadour style.

"Maybe there's too much of it," Mom recently complained.

That day it looked more like she was trying to hold her head together with her hand than using her hand to hold up its burden of hair as she put the hair pins back in. "I suspect that weight is what's been giving me headaches."

On this particular day, while bending over the washtub, she seemed more conscious than ever of that heavy load of hair.

"Juanita, go visit Mrs. Etienne while I go to town," she said as she turned off the fire under the pot of clothes. Mom took a scarf out of her bureau drawer and marched off.

When she returned, she looked different. Her hair wasn't piled on top of her head any more but you could still see a bit of her neck above her collar.

She noticed right away that she did have fewer headaches after that.

"I still have a couple of headaches now and then," she told Dad at supper later that week. She looked at Walt and Dick. "But the barber won't take them like he took my hair."

Mom and Dad laughed together.

"I don't see what's so funny," Dick muttered.

The next day, Dick dashed in to where Herb and Walt were taking turns listening to Herb's radio.

He looked excited and very pleased with himself so Herb took the earphones off his head.

"Today, when Mom took me to help her carry groceries home," he panted, "we went past the minister's house." He dropped down on the nearest chair. "I saw that Mom was holding down her scarf so the ends of her hair wouldn't show. It looked like Reverend Dystant might be home. So I thought I ought to whistle a cheery tune.

"Well, Reverend Dystant came out. He must have been trying to write his Sunday sermon because he started to complain about the noise. I didn't know what noise. I was just whistling. But he sees Mom and that scarf couldn't cover enough.

" 'Mrs. Muller?' " Dick mimicked the minister. " 'You bobbed your hair! What next? Are you going to bob your skirt like all those loose women?'

"Mom just looked at Reverend Dystant. And then she gave me that look of hers. And then she looked back at the minister and says fast as Morse code, 'Good morning, Reverend Dystant. How are you? We're on our way to get groceries. We'll see you in church.' "

After the guffaws died down, Dick rubbed his shoulder and complained with a grin, "It still hurts from when she grabbed me to get us going again. I think she dug in all five fingernails."

"Do you blame her?" Herb asked, as they all started laughing again.

14. Physical Culture

In May of 1925, the Rackham Golf Course opened. It was less than two miles away along the Ten Mile Road where the zoo was taking shape. Herb started caddying there as an extra job.

A doctor he caddied for started calling him Eagle Eye. It was very rare that he wasn't able to follow the ball and then find it, even in the rough. He often was given bigger tips than was usual for caddying. As usual, he saved nearly all that he earned.

Dad saved some money, too. After two years at Ford, Dad was able to buy — no, not his own car — but something even better in Mom's eyes.

"Did you get a delivery today, Clara?" Dad called out when he came home one afternoon.

Mom hurried from the kitchen and pulled Dad through the house back into the kitchen. The boys and Juanita were already there admiring the addition.

"Oh, Herm, it's beautiful," she touched the smooth varnished wood.

70

"I'm sorry I couldn't get one of the deluxe models for you," Dad said. "Some of them had five doors."

"Just having an icebox is a luxury, Herm," Mom squeezed Dad's arm. "The butter will stay cold longer. And with it in the kitchen, I won't have to go down to the basement as much."

"You mean *we* won't have to," Walt pointed at himself and Dick.

"And *you*," Dad laughed and pointed at Walt and Dick, "won't have to go into the basement to empty the water from it either."

There was a dishpan below the tub to catch the water as the ice melted but they soon noticed that it didn't melt as fast in the box because of the tin that lined its thick wooden walls.

The area was growing fast, especially Leggett Farms subdivision and Oak Park Village. As many as three houses went up on each of their subdivision's fourteen blocks every year.

Jefferson School went up west of them. When it opened, Dick and Juanita went there. It was closer, but not by much. Walt was now at Lincoln High.

Juanita's new friend on their block was Mildred DeMay. She was older so she was allowed to go farther by herself. Also because she was older, Mom allowed Juanita to go with her.

Mildred came by often with the invitation, "Let's go to Kelliher's and I'll buy you a Clark bar."

"I don't know where she gets the money, but I do like Clark bars," Juanita told her brothers.

Their church was growing, too. In November, they dedicated an auditorium, which was the temporary sanctuary, and a fellowship room. The gymnasium was already fully scheduled in the evenings. Walt and other boys signed up for a half-hour each of physical culture, basketball and volleyball on Tuesdays.

"They work us hard with those exercises for the first half hour. But it's worth it to play basketball," Walt told the family at supper one Tuesday. "I'm getting much better on account of the practice. I'm sure I'll get to play on the high school team."

Men used the gymnasium on Thursdays, but Dad said he had all the "physical culture" he needed at work. Mondays were for girls and ladies. The Boy Scouts held drills and signal practice on Thursdays and the Epworth League, also for boys, used it on Fridays. On Saturdays, there was a film and recreation night and Walt's favorite, basketball.

On those Wednesday evenings that Dad didn't work, he and Mom went to church and took Juanita with them. The boys were supposed to be doing their homework.

In the evenings when Dad wanted to relax, he'd pull out his guitar.

"Where are you, Girlie?"

As Juanita and Dad started to sing, "Carry Me Back to Ol' Virginny," Dick and Walt groaned and fled outside.

"They're just jealous," Dad said the first time they ran out.

Juanita believed that. She'd sat next to them in church and knew they didn't get the Muller family musical ability. Although she didn't like singing in front of others, but she always liked to sing with Dad.

Dad bought a used player piano. It came with a wooden box filled with rolls of music. It was amazing to watch the keys move after they placed the dowel of a roll on the hooks behind the sliding doors. The family favorites were the "St. Louis Blues" and "Yes We Have No Bananas" and the Sousa marches. Walt sang loudest to "Let Me Call You Sweetheart."

"That sure won't get you any sweetheart," Dick laughed.

Dick liked to sit on the bench and pretend he was playing. Juanita, however, started taking lessons. She babysat for her piano teacher in exchange for lessons. Dick started playing the cornet in school. He wasn't the only happy one in the family when he gave it up.

"Let's go get a ginger ale on Saturday," Dick suggested.

"That's a great idea. I can taste it already," Walt agreed.

"So long as it doesn't look like it'll rain, I'll go, too" Herb said.

They left at 7:00 A. M. in order to be back before dark. Their destination was the Detroit River. Even though it was eleven miles each way, it was worth it for the taste of the Vernor's ginger ale they bought at the factory at the bottom of Woodward. There was nothing else like it.

Herb became active in Hi-Y in his sophomore year in high school. It met at the school. Its goal was "To create, maintain and extend throughout the school and community, high standards of Christian character" through "Clean Living, Clean Speech, Clean Athletics and Clean Scholarship." That was printed on the high school football schedule that year but all Walt saw were all the places he would get to go, too, when he'd be on the basketball team.

"Look! Ypsilanti, Mt. Clemens, Northville. And Monroe, which is almost fifty miles away," he crowed.

"You'll be doing homework on the train," Mom forewarned.

Juanita was pleased to be in the May Day dance around the maypole.

"And I won a first place ribbon for running in the Field Day, Dad," reported Dick.

"Running to or running from?" Dad asked.

15. Jobs

After he worked for Sam Sabaugh for a year, Herb began working for Sam's brother. Charles owned Leggett Farm Dairy Products.

His first job for Charles Sabaugh was candling eggs. By that time, candles weren't used any more. An electric light was placed in a tin can and the egg held up to a hole in the side of the can.

Herb peered through the shell of each egg. If he found a red spot, that egg went into the basket that went to restaurants for baking. It was still a good egg but a customer might not like to find that spot on his breakfast plate. All it meant was that a rooster had fertilized the egg before the hen laid it, though it certainly didn't look like the beginning of a baby chick.

Mr. Sabaugh operated his butter and egg business from the basement of his home four blocks from the Mullers. Herb sometimes went with him to Marine City at the base of the Michigan thumb area to buy eggs from the farmers.

"What do you know about driving, Herb?" Mr. Sabaugh asked on Herb's first trip with him.

"I've watched Uncle Tom and Reverend Cryderman when we rode with them," Herb pointed to the floor at Mr. Sabaugh's feet. "The pedal on the right is the brake. In the middle is the reverse. On the left is neutral until I'd step on it and then it goes forward. Faster if I press it down more, past the other neutral space on it. The stick by your door is the parking brake."

"And very important. I've heard about men getting run over by their own cars because they didn't put it on before they cranked the car. Now tell me about these two levers on the steering wheel."

"The one on the left is the spark advance. It has to be almost all the way down to retard the spark."

"That's correct. That loud backfire we all hear too often is when the driver hasn't learned how much to reduce the spark. That takes practice, Herb."

"And the lever on the right is the throttle to control how fast we go."

"It'll take quite a lot of experience before you get the feel of the throttle for the right amount of fuel. How about starting the car?"

"I'd have to pull the wire loop of the choke to give it a little gas before I crank it."

"Yes and I'll tell you a little trick to keep yourself from getting a broken arm. Don't hold the crank like you'd hold a baseball bat. Tuck your thumb out of the way when you crank it."

There was usually one flat tire, if not two, on every trip. The tire was taken off and the inner tube removed to look for the leak. To make sure the suspicious spot was a hole, one of them spit on it and squeezed the inner tube a little. If bubbles came up through the spit, that was the leak. Or one of them.

Mr. Sabaugh showed Herb how to take the rubber patch from its can, take off the paper that covered the glued side and rough up that side with the metal grating on the end of the can. Then he applied the patch onto the tire where the leak was and rubbed it on with the edge of the can.

"My business is doing so well that I can finally move it out of my basement, " Mr. Sabaugh announced to Herb on one trip for eggs. "I found a building on the Nine. But I'll have to mind the store. Do you think you could drive this truck for me?"

"Yes, sir. Since I've been able to sit in the front seat on our rides, I've learned a lot more by watching you."

"Well, Herb, how about I let you try to drive it once we get out into the country today?"

"Yes, sir!"

Within a week, Herb got a chauffeur's license so he could drive the truck. Mom went with him to give proof that he was fourteen. He paid fifty cents and then the license was his for life, as long as he didn't get into a collision.

Herb came in just before supper one evening.

"You won't believe what happened today. I almost didn't believe it." His eyes were opened wide as if he could see whatever it was happening all over again.

"Thank heavens you survived whatever it was," Mom said.

"I was thanking heaven, too, afterward." Herb continued, "I went up to Marine City for Mr. Sabaugh as I usually do on Thursdays. I was coming back from the farmer's so I was still on a rough dirt road.

"I heard and felt a big THUMP. Then I saw one of my back wheels rolling away *in front of* the truck." Herb gaped in imitation of his reaction earlier that day. "I stopped the truck, got out and ran after it."

"Did you catch it? How'd you get home?" asked Walt.

76

"Of course I caught it. What happened was that a couple of lug nuts broke off the hub. The wheel twisted away and from the grip of the good lug nuts."

"So what did you do?" asked Juanita.

"Well, I jacked up the car, found the good lug nuts and spaced them on the wheel so they would hold it on. Then I drove slowly and extra carefully to the nearest place where I could get more lug nuts."

He smiled broadly. "When I checked, not one of the eggs had broken."

For a while, Dick delivered the *Detroit News* six days a week. He earned fifty cents a week and a free paper every day. Dad read the funnies to them. They all liked "Mutt and Jeff" the best.

Walt began caddying, too. When they didn't have customers, all the caddies went swimming in the pool on the land where the zoo was being built. Skinny-dipping meant that they didn't need to bother with swim trunks. And that meant that there wouldn't be any girls around.

Prohibition had been the law since before they left Missouri. Everyone knew that criminal gangs grew stronger with the money they made from running rum from Canada across the Detroit River. It made newspaper healdines when members of rival gangs killed each other.

Dick walked with Walt to the golf course some mornings for something to do. He did his paper route in the afternoons.

"Guess what we saw this morning?" Walt asked at supper one evening.

"I think I would rather not," Mom said. His tone of voice and the level of excitement both boys showed gave her reason enough to decline the offer.

"It looked like there was lots of blood all over the street — " Dick volunteered the answer anyway.

"And a clump of white stuff that looked like brains," Walt finished. "I'll bet it was the Purple Gang who did it."

But before Walt finished, Juanita left the table and ran to the bathroom.

From then on, Juanita would not go to sleep until "her boys" were all home at night.

Later that September, Herb listened to his radio and tried to relay to his brothers the action in the boxing championship fight broadcast from Philadelphia between Jack Dempsey and Gene Tunney. It was hard to talk and listen at the same time. At the least, he was able to make out that Tunney kept his world heavyweight title, and by a decision rather than a knockout after ten rounds.

"Herb, I saw June Waugh today. She said her Dad just opened his own radio shop," Dick announced. June Waugh had been a classmate of Dick at Washington School and she lived on Marshall, on their way to church. "Let's go tomorrow and see how much the tube radios are."

Ray's Radio was on Marshall halfway to Woodward. June was in the shop, helping her father. On one wall was a framed photograph of a man and two women, one of them standing behind a blond little girl and all four standing in a vegetable garden in front of two large army tents.

"That's what we lived in when we moved to Ferndale in 1918." June stood taller as she added, "We were the fiftieth family to move in."

"And that little girl in the picture is June," Mr. Waugh said. "That's her mother and my older brother and his wife. We came down here from Traverse City for that five dollar day. I worked for Ford for awhile, like your father does."

"Why don't you still work for Ford?" Herb asked.

"I didn't want to have to go all the way to the new Rouge Plant. And I heard it was being run differently than the Highland Park plant."

From money he'd saved from working, Herb bought his first tube radio from Mr. Waugh. Now the whole family could hear the radio at the same time and they didn't need the earphones any more.

16. Changes and Change Over

Henry Ford once said, "People can have the Model T in any color — so long as it's black."

By October 1926, over fourteen million Model Ts had rolled off the assembly lines at Highland Park and the new plant along the Rouge River.

Despite yearly improvements in function, safety and comfort, the Chevrolet Company was catching up to the Ford Motor Company in sales.

Mr. Ford finally gave in to popular demand in 1925 and began to offer the Tin Lizzie in colors. That concession wasn't enough.

Chevrolet had been regularly changing models and finally Henry Ford yielded to pressure to build a new model.

"They'll gradually close down the plants as they stop making Model T's," Dad reported. "They won't open up again with a full workforce until they start the new model. In between, only those men they need for installing the new machines and tools for the new model will have jobs. That'll be mostly the skilled trades so it won't include me.

"But," Dad paused and put a hand on Mom's shoulder, "Ira Walker down the street told me that the Hudson Motor Car Company would be glad to get experienced workers. So I plan to apply as soon as I get the news that Ford won't need me for awhile."

Dad was able to get a job in the Hudson factory for most of the eleven months and seven days that Ford was on changeover. It didn't pay quite as well but he felt fortunate to have a job.

"Earlier this year, the Hudson Company bragged about turning out more automobile engines in an hour than Ford. But that's only because they're doing what Henry Ford came up with for building cars—the assembly line with everything you need: men, materials and machine tools, all in a row." Dad still considered himself a Ford man, and when the plant reopened, he planned to go back.

For caddying, Herb was paid seventy-five cents for each round of eighteen holes. On one Sunday that summer, he caddied four rounds. With tips, he made more money than Dad usually made in a day now. As good as he felt about the money he earned that day, he knew it would be unkind to mention it at home.

In April of 1927, there was an election to make the Village of Ferndale into a city. The first mayor elected was the father of a friend of Herb. That same year, Ferndale made it into "Ripley's Believe It or Not" cartoons in newspapers across the United States. "Ferndale, Michigan and Glendale, California," it said, "are the largest growing cities of their size" out of all the 48 states, and Ferndale "had the highest per capita number of children of any city."

In May, Charles A. Lindbergh flew across the Atlantic Ocean in the *Spirit of St. Louis*, named for the biggest city in Herb's home state. Herb felt pangs of homesickness, yet pride too. It was as if that plane took the challenge of the "Show Me" motto of Missouri and did exactly that.

After school for the next couple of weeks, the Croton's son, Ray, scooped up Lindbergh Specials— ice cream with whipped cream, nuts and a cherry on top, all for 35 cents. "Lucky Lindy, He's Flying High" was the newest roll of music the Mullers bought for the player piano. The boys already heard Ray Croton play the song on the organ in the Sweet Shoppe.

Memorial Day was a big affair in Ferndale. That year, a boulder was placed in front of Lincoln High School in memory of the seventy-three Ferndale men who served in the World War. Herb couldn't believe that Ferndale had been big enough then to have that many men to give for the cause.

On August 15th, the Leggett Farms subdivision became part of the City of Ferndale. The city started to bring the sewers out to them. Dad saw the machine the workers used to lift up the loosened dirt and toss it onto the lawns that he and his neighbors coaxed from the sandy soil.

"I asked them why they didn't aim that chain so it threw the dirt on the other side where no one lives," he said at supper.

"'Too much trouble,' they told me. So I told them, 'We'll see if it's too much trouble. I'm going down to city hall and hear what they have to say about it.'"

Dad paused for a bite of pork chop. "I came in to change my shirt and grab my hat. When I walked past the workers to go to town, I saw them busy with wrenches, yanking the chain towards the opposite direction."

That was the year that the Nine Mile Road was paved, too. The big trucks dropped their loads at Ridge

Road. The cement was mixed in pint-sized cars that looked like miniature railroad coal cars. There was a track for the cars to roll down to the place where their load was needed. After the workmen went home, Herb saw some boys ride the cars downhill towards Woodward. The workmen likely left the cars up on the hill so the boys could have the fun.

In September, they all heard the rematch between Dempsey and Tunney for the boxing heavyweight championship on Herb's tube radio.

"This is swell," Dick said. "It's much better than having to take turns on those ol' earphones. This guy tells it better than you did, Herb." Dick grinned.

"So then, be quiet so we all can hear him," Herb grinned back.

It was the seventh round. Dempsey had knocked Tunney down.

"1, 2, 3..." Then there was a long pause. The announcer told them that the referee was telling Dempsey to go to a corner.

Finally, came "...4, 5, 6, 7, 8, 9 ... "

"And Tunney is back on his feet," they heard through the speaker.

And Tunney won the match and kept his title. They couldn't believe their ears.

"That wasn't fair," grumbled Dick. "Tunney got too much time to get back up. Dempsey had him."

"Rules are rules," said Walt. "Dempsey didn't go to a neutral corner during the count so the referee stopped until he did and then started counting where he left off. It's like in basketball. We have to follow the rules or be penalized."

Herb deepened his voice. "It's like in life, Dickie."

In October of 1927, for his twelfth birthday, Mom took Dick to downtown Detroit to see *The Jazz Singer*.

When they came home, everyone met them at the door.

"What was it like?" Juanita's eyes shone with curiosity. And envy.

"Lucky you, to get to see the very first talkie," Walt said. "Wish I could've gone."

"You ain't heard nothing yet," Dick said in a strange way.

"He's trying to imitate Al Jolson," Mom explained.

"It was swell." Dick went back to his normal voice. "I didn't have to try to look at the picture and read the words and eat my popcorn all at the same time."

"Hard for you to concentrate on anything else when there's food," Herb said. They all laughed.

For too many days afterwards, they heard Dick say, "You ain't heard nothing yet."

17. Cars and Commencement

It had been nearly five years since Dad came to Detroit to work for the Ford Motor Company and he still didn't have a car.

Jitneys now came down Marshall and could take them all the way to Highland Park. The one Mom rode in most often was a big car with a large back seat. After the door closed, one seat on each side could fold down so that two more people could fit inside.

"Mr. Walker just bought a new car," Herb reported at supper.

"So now he has three cars?" Dad asked. "There are only two drivers in his family." Dad's eyes began to twinkle.

"Well, he said if it's O. K. with you, I could buy his old Model T," Herb said.

"What do you think, Clara?" Dad asked. "Do you think Herb is responsible enough?"

Herb's brothers and sister knew Dad was joking. Mom often said that she didn't know of any young person more responsible than Herb. She usually followed this with one of her looks at Walt and Dick.

"Is it the black one?" Juanita asked.

But before Walt or Dick could say, "That's the only color they come in, Silly," they saw her grinning at them.

"She pulled your legs, boys." Dad laughed. "You got them back with that one, Girlie."

The first thing Herb did with his "new" car was to take everything he could out from under the cowl to see how it worked.

He took out each engine part and gave it a spot on the back porch. Then he examined each one as he cleaned it.

"Mom, why are you letting Herb put that dirty old engine on your back porch?" Walt said. "You never let me work on anything on the porch."

"Herb always finishes what he starts, and *he* is very neat and tidy about it."

By the end of the day, Herb had tuned up the engine and put it back together. Inside the car was a vase to put flowers in, so he did.

The Interurban stopped its daily run at 11 p.m. so when Dad worked the second shift, he took the city bus to the Fairgrounds and then walked the two miles home.

Now Herb was able to pick him up. Herb also drove his car to Highland Park to get groceries at the Ford Commissary and to go to the Ford Bank.

But Herb never drove his car very far. With any Model T, not just the trucks, Herb knew you could count on getting a flat tire on nearly every trip of any length.

During one of the few times he was able to persuade Mom to ride in it, he'd come to a rather steep hill.

"Stop the car." Mom ordered. "I'm going to walk down this hill. I'm not going to go down it in this contraption."

One Sunday morning, they woke up to see the results of yet another Michigan ice storm. Trees branches that hadn't broken under the weight rwith stroked the sky with white lacy fingers. But the sidewalks glistened slick and slippery.

Mom asked Herb to drive Juanita to church that morning. Just before the Tin Lizzie reached the corner, it found a frozen puddle and spun 180 degrees.

Herb was finally able to stop it.

"I'd rather walk, if you please," Juanita climbed out of the car.

In June 1928, Herb graduated in the biggest Lincoln High School class yet—93. Only two were graduated back in 1921.

"Let's see your yearbook, Herb," Dad asked.

"Hi-Y Club, Vocational Club, Chemistry Club, Class Secretary the last two years. So between those and your jobs, that's why I haven't seen much of you," Dad said. His own work also kept him away much of the time.

He handed the yearbook to Mom. "Look at the quote under his picture, Clara."

"Clear is his conscience always," she read aloud.

"Now let's see the Class Will," Walt said. He took the book and flipped the pages until he found it. "Lloyd Thompson, Herbert Muller and Kenneth Emmons will their ability to solve Physic problems to Ed Andrew and Al Ruppert," he read. "I thought these were supposed to be funny."

The senior class trip was to Washington, D.C. Herb still saved most of his money from his jobs, so he had enough of his own money so he could go without working on the fundraisers, too.

The best part of the trip was the long train ride. It brought back memories.

One evening, Dick asked at supper, "What month is it?"

"July, of course. Who is being *silly* now?" Obviously, Juanita never forgot the many times that Dick called her that.

"Today I saw something that made me think it had to be October already. Somebody's put a car on top of the office at Wetmore's Service. So I thought Halloween had to be around the corner."

Dick always did have a good imagination. That was Dad's word for what Mom called lies. But for those kinds of "lies," Herb could see the light dance in Dick's eyes and see the corners of his mouth twitch. Neither symptom was there this time. But he had to know it wasn't autumn.

"I'm from Missouri," Dad said. "Show me."

Herb went along to see, too.

Sure enough. There was a Wills St. Claire with its front wheels dangling over the office roof and spinning crookedly. A sign below it asked "Does Your Car Do This?"

"People are calling that the Wetmore Wobble," one of the mechanics told them.

Herb took a course in basic drafting in downtown Detroit. Then, at one company, he worked on the blueprint of a design.

"We work on this huge table. It's four feet by sixteen feet," Herb told the family. "The drawings have to be precise down to 1/64 of an inch. "They'll take our drawings to the model maker who will make a car out of clay one-fourth the final size.

"Do you know what a prototype is? It's a full-sized working model made out of the same materials the finished car would be if they choose to go ahead with this design."

In a later report, Herb told how he'd been able to walk through the whole plant to see the prototype as it was being assembled.

Dad was called back to work at Ford's. The new Model A started to roll out of the Rouge Plant faster than Model T's once rolled out of Highland Park.

Dad and nearly everyone else were transferred from the Highland Park Plant to the Rouge Plant, if the Rouge supervisor didn't have them fired first. The Rouge superintendent was rumored to have said, "I don't want any Model T men in my plant."

It took many bus transfers for Dad to get to work now. Herb picked him up whenever he could.

In late 1928, Herb bought his first new car, a gunmetal blue Ford Model A sedan. Henry Ford finally realized people were interested in how the cars looked and rode, not just in reliability and low cost. "Henry made a lady out of Lizzie," the newspapers reported.

The price was $495. Herb had saved the $250 down payment. Dad went with him to the Coté Motor Car Co. on Woodward to sign for it because Herb wasn't quite legal age. Dad knew Herb could be counted on to make the payments to the Universal Credit Company.

Herb drove slowly away from Coté's. "It will take me some practice to get used to this new pedal arrangement," he told Dad.

"Let's see. To make it go forward, I press on the accelerator pedal with my right foot. The brake pedal is now in the middle. I'm told this clutch system will be easier once I get used to it. Once it's in a gear, it's there until I press in on the clutch and change the position of the gear shift lever. I won't miss that 'high-low' pedal's temperament."

The first thing Herb did was to go to Sweeney's Auto Supply to get gas.

"It certainly is an improvement not to need to get everyone out of the front seat to lift it up to put gas in the car," he said, as he pulled in front of Sweeney's.

"And a gas gauge to tell me when I need gas, too, instead of guessing. And a mirror so I can see if anyone's coming up behind me without having to keep turning around."

"Well, son, it seems to me that you like your new car," Dad grinned.

Herb's face reddened. "Thank you for lending me your name to get it."

"Well, son, I didn't have any money to lend, but your credit is as good with me as it will be with Ford someday."

Herb felt the warmth of Dad's pride in him.

The Detroit Zoo officially opened. A few weeks later, Herb drove the family to see it.

"I wonder if these were the lions we'd heard roar a couple years ago," Herb said to Dick and Walt.

They all had a turn to ride Paulina, the elephant. The Detroit Zoo boasted about being the first zoo in America to have moats instead of bars for some of the animals.

In honor of Herb's new car, the Mullers had a garage built.

Now they could play "Annie-Eye-Over." Dick stood on one side of the garage and Juanita on the opposite side. Dick threw the ball over the roof and took off running around the front. If Juanita caught it, she'd run around the back of the garage to tag Dick with it before he could get to her side.

"She runs fast for a girl! She caught me twice already," Dick said.

90

"And I'll catch you *again*, too," Juanita threatened.

Walter and Dick bought a 1919 Model T.

"How do you like my new car?" Walt asked Herb, as he and Dick were washing it.

"*Our* new car," Dick reminded Walt. "Don't forget I paid half the $50 for it."

It took both of them to run the car, too. In the winter, they had to jack it up on a rear wheel before they cranked it. Once it started, Dick eased the jack down while Walt stood ready to jump behind the steering wheel.

"But you're not old enough to drive yet, Dick," Herb said. "Oh, now I get it. You didn't have quite enough in your savings, Walt, did you? And with what Dick spends on food, he wouldn't have had enough either, even if he were old enough. You're each lucky to have the other."

Walt and Dick looked at each other. Obviously that was the first time either of them ever thought of the other that way.

18. Far Away Places

Mr. A. T. Taylor's son-in-law, Bill Rodgers, owned the Ferndale Drug Store as well as one in Royal Oak. He was about to try the restaurant business.

Rodgers' Dutch Mill opened in December on the lot next to the Methodist Church. It advertised itself as "Greater Woodward Avenue's Most Unique Eating Place." The four-story high windmill was visible from a long way as one came down Woodward Avenue. The building's whole north side was a mural painted to show a town in Holland, with windmills and dikes.

"We went there after school today," Walt said. "They decorated it inside like a street with little houses — shingled roofs and all — on one side and each house has a name.

"The only one I can remember is Blue Heaven Mill, because the ceiling is as dark a blue as Herb's car and has stars on it to make it look like a real sky.

"The mural on the back wall makes it look like the street continues a block past Woodward. The waitresses wear these funny white caps. I suppose that's what the Dutch girls wear."

"How's the food?" Dick asked.

"Dee-licious. You'd like it."

"Dick will eat anything," Herb reminded him. "But since you're more particular, then it must be good."

"Especially the sandwiches. And they're planning to have an ice cream contest. They've already invited the dairies from around here, and whoever is eating there that night will get a free taste of each company's ice cream."

"Count me in," Dick said. They all rolled their eyes at him.

"Speaking of delicious," Walt said, "don't you wish those airplanes had flown over here when they were parachuting Butterfingers?" Butterfingers was a new candy bar and that was what the company did to get publicity.

"Sure. Right over West Marshall. That would have been fine with me, too," Dick agreed.

In the summer of 1929, Herb took the family back to Missouri for a visit. Herb's plan was to see Grandma, Aunt Clara and their cousins, and then to drive on to what he still considered his home town—Oronogo. He knew Juanita would want to see Miss Blanche, too.

Before they left, Herman Atkins offered to paint "Ferndale, Michigan" on the spare tire cover on the back. He lived down the street, was Walt's age, and he was the protector of his sister and her friend, Juanita. Despite being as burly as an Irish cop, he did a very neat job.

"That's so people in Missouri will know how far you've come to see them," he said. The Atkins family also came from Missouri but from a town that was over a hundred miles down the Mississippi River from St. Louis.

Herb strapped the luggage to the running board of the car on the driver's side. In order to get out, he crawled out the passenger door. To get all six of them in the car, Juanita sat in the middle of the front seat. Even a thick pillow didn't keep her from feeling the heat from the exhaust manifold beneath her.

The trip to Missouri took two days. They stayed in a tourist home in Illinois going out and in another one coming back. Both of these were run by widows whose children had grown up and moved out so their former bedrooms were available to travelers at fifty cents a night. The Mullers could see the photographs of the family as they walked past the parlor.

Herb knew when they were approaching the Mississippi River. He saw the high bluff upon which the city of St. Louis reigned. He stroked the rolling hills of Missouri with his eyes and sighed with contentment.

"Look! Paw paws!" Dick pointed at the trees with their long pods dangling like Christmas ornaments.

As they approached St. James, Dad said, as if to himself, "Mother is 84 now."

Herb sensed that the unspoken part of that was Dad's concern that Grandma wouldn't be around much longer. It certainly was part of Herb's reason to take the family on this trip.

Grandma met them in her rocker under the tree. To Herb she looked almost the size of one of Juanita's dolls. She seemed to be tinier than he remembered; he knew the rocker hadn't grown bigger. Her smile was wide and her eyes glowed with a warm light as she turned her arms on the rocker's arms so her hands were palm up as they neared her.

Aunt Clara didn't bustle around quite as quickly but she still baked anise cookies for them.

"You look as though you've haven't starved for cookies, Dick. But now that you're older, can I trust you to carry these for the trip to Oronogo?" She winked at Dad, who grinned back.

"Those cookies will have all the bodyguards they need, Clara," Dad said.

"The fox guarding the henhouse, Dad," said Herb. "I'd vote for Juanita to hold them. At least they'd be up front with the driver."

Oronogo looked more like the ghost town that it had begun to be after the mines were emptied, but it was still Herb's hometown. Despite the passage of six years, much of it was the same. The cherry tree still thrived in front of their old house. But the fruit of the persimmon tree tasted even better than he remembered.

Mom, Dad and Juanita stayed at the Sunday School teacher's home and the boys were invited to stay at the butcher's house.

Miss Blanche didn't look much different than when they left.

"Juanita? My little Juanita?" Miss Blanche didn't need to reach down to give her a hug. Juanita was now as tall as Miss Blanche and looked almost grown up, too. "Do we still have tea parties? I suppose so, but with bigger guests instead of dolls now."

"And real tea, too," Juanita smiled, without her usual shyness.

19. The Not-so-Great Depression

October 29, 1929. The stock market crashed on Wall Street in New York. Herb wasn't sure what that meant. Dad tried to explain.

"There are 'boom and bust' cycles all the time. Everyone invests and builds and buys. Then for some reason, someone gets scared that things are going too far and too fast and panics. More people start selling stocks than buying them so the price goes down. Then the companies have less money to expand. That puts everything in reverse and there's a depression.

"Your grandparents said there was a depression in the 1870s and we had a bit of one in the early 1920s. We lived through them. This is just the biggest drop the stock market has ever experienced so people are as scared as if it's the end of the world."

Dad paused. "At Ford, they're reminding us that because Mr. Ford himself and his family own the company and it isn't in any stock markets, they believe he can ride out whatever comes and keep us working."

Ford still had lots of orders for its new Model A. Other manufacturers were laying off but not the Ford Motor Company.

"Not yet, anyway," worried Mom.

The Ford Motor Company did hold out longer than other automobile companies. But even it became affected. The more people who lost their jobs, the fewer customers there were. Eventually Dad and others began working only three days a week.

The depression deepened into the Great Depression.

Rodger's Dutch Mill closed. People could barely afford food to cook themselves. Eating at a restaurant became a luxury.

"I guess now Betty Taylor won't be able to go to the Ferndale Theater much either. Mr. Ealand used to trade rolls of tickets with her Daddy for meal tickets," Herb said.

"Lucky. I'll bet she got to see every one of the Tarzan pictures," Dick complained.

"Well, we were pretty lucky, too," Juanita reminded him. "Herb gave us each a dime and took us to the movie on his own birthday."

Banks collapsed. Anyone who had money in one of the banks that failed now had only useless paper to show for their deposits. The Ferndale Savings Bank, where the Mullers had a small savings account, closed.

"Can't say we lost much but it was all the rainy day money we had," Dad said.

The church's mortgage of $27,000 was held by the Ferndale Savings Bank. The bank's creditors were calling in all debts and that included mortgages. The bank's creditors sued the church on its mortgage.

The judge allowed church members to bring in their Ferndale Savings Bank passbooks and any other claims they had against the bank to offset the balance owed by the church. In just two weeks, they were able to collect enough of them to pay off the church's mortgage.

"Well, at least our bank passbook was able to help the church," Mom said.

"The Muller's mite, but better than having nothing to show for it," Dad agreed.

Mom worried about the coal bills every winter, but the winter of 1929-1930 was much colder than usual.

It was also a particularly heavy snow year. The zoo had to use the elephants to haul in the hay for the animals because the trucks couldn't get through.

"And they're Ford trucks, too," Dad chuckled, somewhat grimly.

Then, by the hundreds, many of the Ford Men lost their jobs entirely. All those who once worked at the Highland Park plant were the first to go. It didn't matter that they had been Ford Men longest. Dad was among them.

Then even the Rouge plant was for the most part shut down, with nearly everyone laid off until the remaining company officials were sweeping floors. Because so many people were out of work and no one had enough money to buy even the necessities, Dad couldn't get much work anywhere and nothing full-time. He was paid much less per hour than he'd earned before with Ford.

Mr. Lathers managed the Leggett Farms subdivision properties. Herb answered the door when Mr. Lathers came by one evening and asked for Dad and Mom. The three of them spoke on the porch.

Herb, who was at his radio at the dining room table couldn't hear what was said but noticed his parents looked both sad and relieved when they came back in.

"Herb, we know you understand what's going on," Dad began. "Since you graduated, we know you've been staying around to help us."

Herb started to object. "What I understand is that times are so bad I couldn't afford to live anywhere else." He smiled.

Mom smiled back, with sadness and affection mixed together. "Herb, we appreciate all you're doing. So you might as well know how things stand."

"We've gotten behind on the mortgage payments," Dad said. "Mr. Lathers was here to tell us that he has to foreclose on us. But there was a bit of good news. Before he came, he figured out how much ownership equity we accumulated from our six years of payments. We can stay until that's used up. It will give us until next summer."

"Things are sure to get better by then, Dad."

20. Fun and a Funeral

They didn't.

Very slowly, Ford called men back. Uncle Tom went back to work at Ford's but not in as good a job as he'd had before.

"But at least it's work," he told them at Easter. "We got very behind on the house payments. We're still not out of the woods."

As summer approached, Mom's worry about where they were going to live had risen inside her like the yeast rising in her bread dough.

Early one morning, she pushed her hat on her head with the force she usually used to punch into the dough. She used the released energy to hunt for a house for them to rent.

Herb started to say, "Mom, would you like me to drive you?" but she was out the door before he said the second word.

"I found a house," she reported that evening. "It's of course somewhat smaller than this one." She looked around the table. "It's across Woodward at 400 E. Drayton." Still, no one looked up. She slowed and tried a cheery, "It's much closer to the Interurban stop."

"To go where?" Dad mumbled. "No job."

Moving out of the house on Marshall was a big blow to Dad.

"Going backwards," he said. "I'm not alone but that's little consolation."

Uncle Tom soon became afraid that he, too, was going to lose his cherished house. He jumped into the Detroit River from the Belle Isle Bridge. The Coast Guard threw him a life preserver and he refused it.

Uncle Tom was only 60 years old.

On the day of the funeral, Mom tried to sit up tall but most often leaned on Dad. Herb saw that Dad had brought extra handkerchiefs, and had put them in a pocket he could get at with the hand that wasn't holding Mom next to him.

"My dress looks pretty on you, Mildred," Juanita said. Mildred didn't have a dress nice enough to wear and Dad suggested Juanita loan her cousin the newest one he had bought his Girlie.

Mildred didn't answer. It looked to Herb as if she hadn't even heard Juanita. The expression on her face was almost no expression at all.

They went to Uncle Tom's house after the funeral.

Their cousin Paul spoke slowly and almost in a whisper, as if the words were hard to form. "I'd gone that day to Farmington to look at a new house for Mom and Dad." He looked up. "It had a large garden in back for Dad." He looked back down at his knees.

"It was to be a surprise. Something told me to go back that morning," he looked up to the ceiling, as if pleading to have time turned back. "But I couldn't think of why," his voice caught. "So I didn't." Paul put his head into his hands.

Herb put his hand on Paul's back and left it there a long time. He couldn't imagine losing his own Dad.

The big black funeral hearse carried Uncle Tom's coffin to the Evergreen Cemetery on Woodward just south of the Eight Mile Road.

Every Sunday after the funeral, Mom walked to the cemetery to visit Uncle Tom's grave. Nearly every Sunday, Grandma Myers walked with her, to visit the grave of her son, Carl.

Directly across from their new home was the new Coolidge School, named after another President of the United States.

"One who is still living," Herb pointed out. Washington, Jefferson and Lincoln Schools were all named after presidents who died a long time ago."

Coolidge Elementary School went up to the eighth grade and Juanita was just starting into the seventh.

"I'm glad we moved here, Nita," Dick said. "I told Mom I didn't want us to live where you'd go to junior high where I was going to high school."

"So what are you doing at the high school that you don't want me to see? I'm no tattletale anyway." Juanita shoved her hands onto her hips and stuck her chin out in his direction.

"Well, maybe not anymore," Dick grinned and stepped back.

Actually, Dick had the most fun living here. Because they lived across from the school and its large playground, there were many more kids to run around with than on Marshall.

Dick spent most of the time during his high school years with neighborhood friends. Two of Dick's best friends were Don Daly and Joe McCain. Both went to St. James Catholic Church, which was in the block next to their Methodist Church, but Joe also went to St. James' high school.

Don and Joe were often around the house when Herb came home from work at the A & P Grocery Company in Berkley.

Dad was on the front porch watching the boys play wheelie lath in the street as Herb came home one evening.

"When I was a boy, we played that, too," Dad called out. "But we had wobbly wagon wheels instead of smooth automobile wheels. And we used small tree branches instead of smoother pieces of lathing. You boys have it easy!"

"Aw, it's still hard enough, Dad," Dick protested, as he wielded the three-foot lath atop the spoked wheel to keep the wheel upright and headed in the direction of his foe.

Don, Dick, Walt and Joe darted at each other and each tried to knock down another's wheel while keeping his upright.

Marble tournaments were popular. The boys drew lines on the street or sidewalk in the shape of triangles or circles with a two-foot diameter. One boy's agate was put inside and then another boy aimed his marble at it to shoot it out of the figure. If he succeeded, he got to keep it. They all became such good shots that the aggies were passed around frequently.

Juanita and her new girlfriends played hopscotch or swung on the swings behind the school until dark.

"Why do the boys get to stay out after dark? It's not fair!" Juanita said.

"It's those roughhousing boys we're protecting you against. Remember that two of them are your own brothers!" Mom knew, though, that Walt and Dick wouldn't let harm come to Juanita. "I'm sorry, Juanita. Boys always seemed to have more fun when I was a girl, too."

"Girlie, let's you and I sing," Dad said and pulled out his guitar.

Herb could read his technical books and ignore the noise around him but Dad's music made a pleasant background sound for studying.

After two months, the real estate agent who managed his company's rental properties in Ferndale came by one evening.

"We told him we didn't have the rent money right now," Dad said at supper. "I tried to tell him we'd have it soon but he interrupted me.

" 'You and I both know that times are hard for everybody,' he said to us. 'I know you'll pay when you can. In the meantime, I'm authorized to permit good families like yours to stay as long as you take care of the place. We've lost some houses to vandalism after we've evicted people and that costs the company more than unpaid rent.' "

"And so," Mom said, "I know I don't need to tell you that we will do exactly that. We will take better care of this place than if we owned it."

"What's better than perfect, Mom?" Dick acted as if that were an innocent question.

Even Mom joined in the laughter. Despite three boys and all their friends running in and out, Mom's housekeeping was enough to make a hospital envious. A sigh of relief exhaled with the guffaws and broke the tension for that evening at least.

"We pulled one on the cops tonight," Dick said to only Walt and Herb. "You know how they keep chasing us off the school grounds at night?"

He looked down in thought for a moment. "I don't know why. We're not doing any harm." He looked up.

"Anyway, we strung a clothesline across the alley about ankle high. We knew where it was so we could hop over it. But they didn't. We could hear them cussing as they got all tangled up."

"Ahem," Herb cleared his throat in the way Dad did to begin scolding. Then he laughed, too, at the picture in his mind. He'd never heard of any vandalism at the school either.

A few weeks later, Dick had another story to tell.

"They got one on us this time."

"Who did?" Walt asked.

"The *po*-lice." Dick drew out the word, and the story, until he got Herb's full attention. "You know the bushes at the back of the school? Well, the cops chased us through those. Except we didn't *get* through." Dick shook his head in wonderment and admiration. "They'd strung a clothesline right through them and caught us all." Dick laughed with his brothers.

After the laughter subsided, Walt asked, "So why aren't you in the hoosegow?"

"You're lucky you aren't. You know there's no extra money to bail you out," Herb said.

"Aw, this stuff is just a game. They know it. We know it. We all had a good laugh and then they pretended to 'give us a warning.' "

Halloween was somewhat different during the depression. Witches and hoboes used to call out, "Help the poor" as they held open their paper bags, but this year it was for real.

No one could afford to give out candy so oranges, apples and potatoes were dropped into the sacks of the ghosts and goblins. Fruit was indeed a treat these days and Mom was glad of it, too.

There was another way in which Halloween was different in Ferndale.

"The men at church said that Chief Reynolds' plan to prevent the usual destructive Halloween pranks worked," Dad said. "Not that any of our boys were affected by it," he looked at Walt and Dick.

105

"You know we weren't one of those who did that," Walt protested. "With our parents, we wouldn't dare!"

"But I didn't mind helping myself to the cider and to the hot dogs the policemen were cooking," Dick said. "In fact, I went to two of those places because they weren't giving out seconds yet at the first one."

"They've got your number, Dick," Dad grinned. "Feed you and you'll stay out of trouble."

21. Will Work for Food

Mom and Dad were on the front porch. Walt and Dick were on the back porch. Juanita was in the backyard picking chrysanthemums for the table.

"I'm hungry," Dick said. "Where's Herb?"

"Here I am." Herb came around the house from the driveway. Saturday night supper waited until he came home from work with the groceries that he took as part of his pay.

"I almost forgot how annoying little sisters could be," Dick raised his voice so Juanita could hear.

Juanita ignored him.

Dick shrugged. "But I was reminded today. Joe and I were over at his girlfriend's house. Victoria's sister Georgette is nine. She overheard us talking about Dad not being called back by Ford yet. 'My Daddy was smarter than your Daddy,' she said."

" 'Oh, yeah?' I said.

" 'Oh, yes.' she said. 'He quit working at Ford. They didn't let anyone go to the toilet if it wasn't lunchtime.

So he quit. And he bought himself a grocery store. Everyone *always* needs groceries. *Not* everybody needs those noisy old cars.' What a brat."

It was quiet for a moment as Dick sulked.

Then Herb softly said, "Dick, she made a good point. I'm lucky to work for a grocery store. And luckier that it's a chain store. They're more able to stick out a depression than some of the family-owned stores even like Yezbick's."

Herb was worried about Dad. For a short while, Dad worked at the city yard in Ferndale. His job was smashing cans.

Herb and his brothers put their heads together to find ways for Dad to feel productive. Since Dad liked to grow things, they set him up to grow mushrooms in the basement. They were able to sell some, including to Mr. Yezbick's store. They talked Dad into making plaster cast elephant bookends. There wasn't much of a market for them but it kept him busy.

In the winter or bad weather, all of them, including Juanita, played Ping-Pong on the dining room table. Once they pulled the table out all the way for a birthday party for Dick's friend, Joe.

Often right after supper, Dad played chess with any available young man.

"Put 'em away," he barked, after losing a game.

Then later in the evening, he'd come back to the table. "Set 'em up. I'm going to beat you this time."

Walt graduated from high school in 1931. Because the classes started saving for the senior trip in their freshman year, his class already had most of the money before times became hard. They were able to take their senior trip to Washington, D.C.

In his yearbook, the quotation by his photograph was, "A man of few words."

"And uses them often," Dad laughed. He occasionally called Walt his "Gabby Gus."

"And now the Class Will," Dad turned a few pages. The Depression did affect the yearbook. It was quite slim with a thin paper cover. It didn't contain photographs of other classes or of student activities as the others had. It took only a few seconds for Dad to find what he was looking for.

"Walter Muller and Robert Templin will their ability to keep their emotions and expressions under control..." Dick started to guffaw as Dad tried to keep his own face expressionless, "...to Karl Kauffman and Lawrence Galbreath."

"Now that's the way yearbooks are supposed to be!" Dick pointed at Walt.

Like Herb, Walt joined Hi-Y and the Vocational Club, although for only two years. It would have been no surprise to anyone who knew him that basketball was listed for all four years. In his senior year, he was on the reserve team.

"We won eight out of fourteen games and lost four of them by only a few points each," Walt boasted.

Later that summer, at supper time, the doorbell rang.

"Western Union. For Daddy," Juanita called back from the door.

Dad found something for a tip for the man, took the telegram and walked slowly to a chair.

No one spoke as he sat down. He read the telegram aloud, slowly, shaking.

"Mother dying. STOP. Doctor says only days left. STOP. Albert."

Mom quietly pushed her chair away from the table and went to him. She put a hand on his shoulder.

A few minutes passed. Dad looked up.

"It's good that we saw her when we went back to Missouri." He looked at Herb.

Dad looked down at the telegram again but not as if he saw it. "I hoped that wouldn't be the last time..." his voice trailed off.

The four of them at the table looked at each other.

In a low voice, Herb said, "I'm going to the corner to use the telephone. I'll find out how much a train ticket costs."

Then louder, he said, "Excuse me."

"We'll go check our piggy banks," Walt said quietly.

They each asked to be excused from the table, to no one in particular. And no one answered.

Herb knew a few people to whom Dad loaned money before the Depression hit him, too. Herb merely told them the news and without saying more, they added what they could.

Mom had just started putting a few coins in her rainy day jar again. They managed to scrape up enough money for Dad to go.

"Stay as long as you need to, Dad." Herb said. "I'll take care of everything here."

"It's not like I have a job to come back to." A grimness at the corners of Dad's mouth added to the sad look in his eyes.

A week later, Mom received a postcard from him. Grandmother died just before he arrived, but he was told that she had smiled when she heard he was on his way.

"Every shop in town closed up for the hour of Mother's funeral," Mom read aloud. "There was a written proclamation from the mayor about how much my parents were esteemed in the town."

Mom looked up. "It is wonderful that the town remembered them in that way."

A couple weeks later, Dad sent a postcard to Juanita.

"Dad's handwriting is so beautiful," she said softly.

St. James Mo
8/ 13-31

Dear Girlie,

*I have not forgotten you. because I did
not write you. and I sure want to see
you all. and will soon.*

Dad.

22. Leave Michigan?!

The American State Bank on the Ferndale side of Eight Mile Road and Woodward collapsed. The institution, that is. The building was still standing.

The City of Ferndale had its bank account there so its funds were frozen along with everyone else's. The city council voted to turn in its account books in exchange for the building. City offices had been getting crowded anyway.

Finally, in 1932, Dad was back working at Ford's. Now they were only paying him fifty-nine cents an hour for the same work he had been earning ninety-two cents an hour for in 1929, just before the crash. And at first it was only for two days a week. Later on it was three.

Henry Ford had started the eight-hour day. He had already shortened the work week from six days to five. Now, even though his workers earned $7 a day, most of them were behind what they'd earned years before because they worked fewer hours a week.

Dad was now working in the steel rolling mills. It was incredibly hot work, even with open windows and the other man on his team pouring the cooling water.

"Did I tell you that they don't throw anything away?" Dad asked.

"After we're done rolling out the big pieces for the body parts, they give us the two-inch thick hunk of steel leftover from the forge. We roll it through each of two smaller mills, like your Mom uses her rolling pin to stretch out and thin her cookie dough..." Dad forced a smile and winked at his middle son, "...when she's not waving it at Walt."

"Mmmmm." Dick rolled his eyes and patted his stomach at the mention of Mom's cookies.

"We roll it through five times until it's a quarter-inch thick. By then it's ten feet long. We put it into the salvage yard." Dad sighed and attempted another smile. "Those sheets of steel are much heavier than the leaves of tobacco I lifted in the factory when we lived in St. Louis."

Dad had been in his middle forties when they moved to Michigan, and didn't act his age then. Now, in his mid-50's, he looked like a much older man than he actually was.

Juanita's eighth grade class graduated from Coolidge. That fall Dick was in his last year of high school.

"So now we're both going to the same school again," Juanita pointed out. "So you'd better behave yourself, because I'll tell!"

"There'll be nothing to tell. When I went to get my hair cut today, Mr. Pankle asked me what I was planning to do after I graduated. He's offered to train me after school to be a barber. I'd get a part of the quarter he charges for men's haircuts."

"And a smaller amount for part of the 15 cents that he charges for children's haircuts," Walt said. "As wiggly as children are, it seems he'd charge more for them."

Mom looked up. "I'm glad he didn't charge more for children. If he had, I would have gotten out a bowl and done yours even after you were in high school."

"Then I'd have borrowed one of your scarves, Mom," Dick said.

She touched the back of her still short haircut, chuckled and shook her head at him.

"Well, now you can do your cutting up and make money at it, too," Herb teased. Yet his tone of voice expressed approval, too.

Herbert Hoover was President of the United States. His campaign slogan in 1928 had been "A chicken in every pot, a car in every garage."

"Clara, can you believe he's running for re-election?" Dad asked. "I have a garage but no car; a pot but no chicken."

"You were smart to have four of us, Dad," Herb grinned. "You not only have our cars in your garage, but you have your own personal chauffeurs."

Dad didn't smile back. He seemed to have lost most of his sense of humor when he lost his job. Only occasionally did a glimmer of it shine up to the surface once Ford Motor Company called him back to work.

Hoover wasn't reelected, even though Henry Ford supported his campaign. The whole country heard the inauguration speech of Franklin Delano Roosevelt on the radio.

"This great nation will endure as it has endured, will revive and prosper." The strength in the new President's voice was a contrast to the despair felt in millions of homes. "The only thing we have to fear is fear itself."

On March 12, 1933, eight days after taking office, FDR had his first "fireside chat." The family gathered

114

around the tube radio for each one of his chats, ears grasping for reasons to hope like a drowning man grabs for a life preserver.

Congress passed fifteen programs to help the "one-third of a nation" that now were poor. One of them was the Public Works Administration. Under the PWA, Dad was hired for one project.

"All I'm doing is shoveling dirt from one place to the other." Dad shook his head. "And then Percy's job is to shovel it right back."

Their church organized a program of its own to aid members and their friends during the depression by providing some food, clothing, and coal.

Congress passed the Home Owner's Loan Act in 1933 to help save thousands from having their houses foreclosed.

"Too late for us and too late for Tom," Mom said. Herb couldn't tell whether Mom's voice expressed bitterness, sadness or hopelessness. Probably it was all three.

Michigan was the first state to ratify the 21st Amendment. After enough other states followed its lead, Prohibition and Beerless Beer Gardens ended on December 12, 1933.

"It doesn't make much of a difference to us," Dad said. "But I'll bet it takes the wind out of the sails of the rumrunners."

"I guess we won't be finding blood and brains on the roadway again," Walt said, as if he were in mourning.

"Good," Juanita said.

For Dick's graduation, there was no senior trip. They were given a "skip day" instead. Boys borrowed their father's cars and packed in their classmates for the organized picnic to Dodge State Park Number 4.

"That's barely farther than when our neighbor took us to Walled Lake for the day," moaned Dick.

"Must be that your whole class is made up of adopted children, to get such treatment," Walt joked.

"At least you and Herb got your senior trips," Dick retorted.

There was practically nothing for most young people to do after high school and certainly no money for further schooling. Youth, Inc. was formed in Ferndale. By collecting certificates just like the Methodist Church had done, they obtained a five-room Cape Cod house from the bank which had taken it back for nonpayment.

Materials were donated and carpenters and others with skills gave many young volunteers on-the-job training while they all remodeled the house. Someone named the new center The Castle on the Nine.

The Castle was finished in 1934. It offered many types of recreation, training in skills and "Intellectually Stimulating Classes" for both males and females, with volunteer teachers and no tuition. A large lighted patio was constructed in the back for dances. That's the part of the place Herb, Dick and Walt liked best.

Finally, the situation began to appear less bleak in general.

"Mom, come see the raise I got," Herb called in the front door early one morning.

"I thought you received a raise three months ago," she said, as she wiped her hands on a kitchen towel and came to the front door.

"Oh, I did. That helped me get enough money quicker."

"Enough money for what? Now what have you…"

"Where do you want us to put this, ma'am?" said one of the two men standing on the porch.

116

Mom's mouth dropped open and the towel dropped to the floor.

Between the two men was a washing machine.

Herb had to answer for her.

Juanita graduated from high school in 1936.

"A smile is worth more than millions can buy" was printed along side her photograph in the yearbook. The activities listed for her were Glee Club, of course, and two musicals, *The Pirates of Penzance* and *The Mikado*. The Class Will informed the reader that "Hazel Lemp, Juanita Muller and Dorothy Moorhead are taking their demureness with them."

"Aw, that's not funny," Dick said.

"Or true either," Walt said. "They don't know our little sister like we know our little sister."

"Obviously, she knows how to act like a lady in public," Mom said, with pride. In fact, for the past few years, Mom had used "that look" at the boys less and less. She had replaced it with looks of pride and of gratitude.

Herb looked around at them all. He'd kept his promise to Dad. He helped take care of the family and now they're all grown.

"I have an announcement to make," Herb said and then was silent.

His mother turned toward him, a questioning look on her face. Even Walt and Dick were quiet. Juanita walked over to him.

"What is it, Herb?" Dad asked.

"I applied to work at Lockheed Aircraft Corporation in California and they want me. Our cousins there offered to let me stay with them. I'll write."

Epilogue

Even as I was writing this, Juanita still believed that Dick had told Mom to move them to where Juanita wouldn't go to the same school he was attending. "I was joking," he said, shaking his head at his sister.

The family lived in the house on Drayton until 1939 when they bought a house on West Troy Street, west of Woodward.

Dad was awarded a 25-year pin for working at Ford, then retired in his seventies. He never owned a car, having raised for himself those four personal chauffeurs. He lived to be ninety. Mom died at home on her 103d birthday.

Grandfather Muller's Civil War uniform and saber is in the Maramec Museum, in St. James, Missouri.

Herb continued to work as a draftsman until his retirement. He traveled to Alaska, Jerusalem and many other places in the USA and the world. In 2000, the Methodist Church threw a big party for his ninetieth birthday.

Walt worked for Weber Brothers Greenhouse for many years. Mr. Weber paid for a one-year short course in floriculture for him at what was then Michigan State College (now Michigan State University). The Webers provided all the flowers for Walt's wedding. He later worked as an auto body painter for Hodge's Dodges, a shop which still exists in Ferndale, although under another name. Walt spent lunch hours helping Mom and Dad. After retirement, he moved to Florida with his beloved wife, Doris.

Dick went into military service during World War II, brought home an Irish bride, Mary. They built their house next door to Mom and Dad. With his wife, he did see the Malamute Saloon in Alaska. They too enjoyed traveling the globe.

Juanita worked first in cosmetology, then as a school secretary. Neither she nor Herb ever married, "though not for lack of opportunities," Herb assured me. ("He was the best-looking one of us all," Dick said.)

Herb and Juanita stayed in the family home on West Troy, taking care of their parents and then each other.

The Methodist Church dedicated a beautiful sanctuary, its final building, in 1951. The Church is still a place for young people to have fun constructively, no matter what religion their families practice, if any. Until 1990, Herb was involved in the youth program, as was Dick for twenty years. Juanita taught Sunday School and played piano.

S. S. Kresge's dime stores eventually grew into the K-Mart chain we know today.

Instead of Coté, Ferndale's Ford dealership is Ed Schmid. One of their sales people, who has sold to the Mullers, is Laura Hess Dill, the granddaughter of the Ferndale policeman who wore badge number two.

Don Daly married Georgette, that little sister of Joe McCain's girlfriend and later wife, Victoria.

119

Long before the author ever heard of Ferndale, she and the Daly's son, Craig, commiserated through law school together. It's a small world.

As Herb wrote, in his contribution to the Ferndale memories that became the seed of this book:

"Time has proven that they were well justified in their decision to come to Michigan. We have had a happy life here and our roots are well established in the soil of Michigan. The two younger generations of our family have no memories of our state of origin and so have no divided loyalties as the older may have had."

I moved in across the street from the Mullers in 1988. Dick and Mary have been "Grandpa and Grandma" to my daughter and Grandpa Dick always has candy in his pocket. In 1999, Herb autographed my copy of the book, *Old Timers tell it like it was.* He asked if I'd like to see the full five pages he wrote "that they *cut* from," and that is what started this book.

As I was finishing my writing, I checked the cars in their driveways.

"All Fords?" I asked Dick.

"Of course," Dick said. "Daddy was a Ford Man."

Juanita
Herbert, Richard, and Walter 1974

Photo and labeling courtesy of Herbert Muller

About the Author

Sherry A. Wells read all the books of the Little House series to her daughter Amanda, and together they visited Mansfield to see the little house in the rolling hills of Missouri where those books were written and DeSmet, South Dakota, where the true stories in most of those books took place.

Amanda's Mom moved to Ferndale in 1988 so Amanda has lived there her whole life. Although the book tells about the First Methodist Church of Ferndale, Amanda and her Mom are Unitarian Universalists and still hope to help establish one of those congregations in Ferndale.

The Mustang was the author's favorite Ford car.

About the Illustrator

Randy Bulla secludes himself in an elevated studio overlooking charming Sylvan Lake in Michigan, coming out occasionally to go for a run or travel to a Formula One race.

Both the author and the illustrator are members
of the
Society of Children's Book Writers and Illustrators.